BROKEN DOLLS:

DELIVERANCE

By Mique Watson

Copyright © 2023 Mique Watson
All rights reserved.

"Hell was all about helplessness, as was the condition of being human."

(Charlee Jacob, 2003)

Broken Dolls: Deliverance

Copyright © 2023 Mique Watson
All rights reserved.

Except for the use of brief quotations in book reviews, no part of this book may be reproduced, stored in a retrieval system, or transmitted in any form by any means without the written permission of the author and publisher.

ISBN: 9798862652505
Imprint: Independently Published
Cover art: Christy Aldridge, Grim Poppy Design
Edited by: Lisa Lee Tone

The events, characters, and locations in this book are all fictional. Any resemblance to reality is unintended and coincidental.

WARNING: This is an extreme horror novel. It features graphic, disturbing, and offensive content. It is not recommended for sensitive readers, or readers under the age of 18.

To anyone who has ever been abandoned.

PROLOGUE

"I started considering my guts were severely mangled about the seventy-third time a monster cock plowed my ass."

The doctor responds with a look of incredulity. His eyes crawl up. What he does next is predictable—as if he's a marionette being manipulated by a puppet master in the shadows. First, the gentle blink toward consciousness. Next, the uneasy cough as he loosens the tie around his neck. And finally, the finger pushing his glasses onto the crook of his nose.

Every time.

"I see. And this number ... these sexual encounters are ones you've been keeping track of?"

"Nah, I think I stopped counting after about the first thirty or so. I pulled that number out of my ass just like the butt plug you used on me last time."

He chokes on his breath.

"Well, I—if you're not going to be completely honest with me, I don't know if there's anything else I can do for you. Why did you come in today?"

I raise my bare foot to Doctor Adler's ankle and find the fleshy patch of skin right beneath the hem of his slacks. He sits there, waiting with bated breath for my response. He swallows a gulp of spit so thick you'd think he'd just had an entire plum in his mouth.

"Oh, Doctor. You called me. You wanted to give me a checkup today ..." I say, raising my foot to his inner thigh now.

"Oh, y-yes." He coughs, adjusting his glasses. "Get on the examination table and we will begin. Take all that off."

I pull my pants down and shrug my shirt over my head. I sit down across from him, leaning back on my forearms and parting my legs, glaring at him. He squints, struggling to maintain eye contact.

"Now what, Doctor?"

He runs two fingers along the pale flesh of my inner forearm.

"Are these new?"

"Be more specific, *Doctor*."

He sighs. "These cuts. I didn't see them before. They look fresh. Did you make them before coming here?"

"Does it matter?"

He straightens and moves his hand to my thigh, lightly grazing the shattered fault lines of my flesh. The smattering of scars and scabs etched on nearly every inch of me surprised him at first, but in the end, I guess they all like damaged goods just the same.

His inquisitive digits find my abs—another mural of cuts. This specific one he's lingering on is old; it says GUTTERSLUT.

"I ..." He coughs.

"Is something wrong, Doctor?"

"I was hoping you could be the doctor today, Adam."

Adam. This old fat fuck can't even use the same name on me. Last time it was Charlie; the time before that, Harold. I wonder what Adam looks like, what fantasy he conjured that name from.

"Fine. Shall I dress up?"

"No, stay as you are ... I'm going to need you to examine me instead."

"All right. Disrobe then."

He starts with that hideous tie. Then the lab gown, then the shirt underneath it. He's kept his clothes on the last few times. This is new. All I'd seen of him the last few encounters was his face shined with grease. His cheeks were adorned with freshly scraped acne scars, his lips so pink they looked like newly thawed beef. The more his clothes shed, the more I am presented with a mural of rot and decay. The rest of his fat body is caked in sweat and grime.

"Take that bottle of oil next to you ... rub it on me, please."

I do as instructed.

His folds are caked with dead skin and mold. Beneath the field of gray hair on his chest is a row of creamy boils ready to burst at any moment. There isn't a single smooth patch of skin to him—something he and I have in common.

"Now, could you ... I mean—"

"Hey, I'm the doctor here."

"Oh. Uh, right."

"I think the problem is that you're backed up. I can sense some buildup right about here," I say as I plant a firm grip on his crotch. This comes with a squelching sound like that of wringing a fistful of newly washed laundry. The air in the room reeks with the stench of debauched anticipation.

"F-fuck," he gasps.

He instantly hardens under my touch.

"Be sure to look into the camera. Novak wants them to see all of this."

~

When I finish, it's still daytime. I'm on my phone with Novak when a beggar taps me on the shoulder and asks me for change. I suppose at one point, I would've sympathized with him and found whatever I could in my pocket. This time, I shrug him off and keep walking near the end of the intersection.

Moments later, a car horn blares ... followed by a loud thud and scrape. I whirl back as a car swerves. It's an old Volvo; its tires screech as it hightails it out of the scene. The beggar's leg is contorted in an act of defiance against his body's ergonomic limits. His arm is folded behind him in a straight line, and his empty eyes glare up at the sky. Blood pools from under his head and drenches his back. If I could use one word to describe him, that word would be *cracked*.

My legs move before my mind has any time to think. I am then over the beggar, pushing his chest and blowing breaths into his mouth. His breath is tinged with the bitter taste of cheap whiskey. A crowd forms around us, but I don't stop.

One, two, three ... One, two, three ... blow.

Is this how CPR is done? I have no fucking idea what I'm doing.

An ambulance arrives.

A flurry of images my mind can't precisely arrange plays out in front of me. The stretcher, the police taking statements, the people staring at us in astonishment ... the flashes of cellphone cameras. A shallow groan morphs into a feral rattle inside his chest.

I'd give anything to switch places with him.

CHAPTER 1: NOW

Joe. Blood. So much blood. Sharp pain jousts through my neck as I lean against the metal tub. The thudding soreness behind my eyes is exacerbated by the dryness of my throat.

My forehead is bespeckled with dried blood over a series of scabbed gashes. My taste buds are tinged with various coppers and irons; any more time spent in this basement and you could probably call me a blood sommelier.

I can't remember the last time Joe showed signs of consciousness. His chest rises; this gives me a small sense of comfort. With what he and I have gone through, I'll take what I can get.

With the amount of bruising and swelling covering Joe's body, I'm amazed he's managed to live this long. Both his eyes are completely bloodshot. His nose is bent, smashed, and caked in clots of blood. His popped lips ooze a mucus-like substance that smells like piss. His right ear has been nearly bitten off; it hangs limp with only scant connective skin.

He's woken up a couple of times since and screamed.

I've tried to calm him, but his eyes could never meet mine. They'd always stared past me.

We weren't the first people in this room. Various limbs, guts, and viscera paint the floor and walls. Dried corpses are hanging from hooked chains on the ceiling. The freshest one is a woman hanging upside down from her ankles; her remaining eye is rolled to the back of her skull, and her fingertips float above a puddle of blood dripping with the sound of a metronome. Ropes of mauve intestines sag between her mauled breasts. The skin of her face has been flayed off.

These rotting corpses emit an odor of shit preserved in embalming fluid. The air inside this basement secretes a wet and sulfuric stench.

All of this hit me at once upon first waking up. I vomited, but the ball gag tightly fastened to my throbbing head pushed all the boiling upchuck back down.

I want to rip out the ball gag and tell Joe I love him. That I'd loved him ever since we were kids. That he is the only person I've ever loved in this world. More than myself even.

Yet his eyes, there is no life left in them. None whatsoever. Pools of blue that are empty. Vacant. Dead.

Joe, I promise I am going to get you out of here. Whatever it takes.

CHAPTER 2: SUMMER OF 2004

By summer's core, the crickets chirped, the white cotton fluttered the air to drizzle on the streets, and the leaves glowed a blistering shade of green. As the sun set, dusk swept its dull lavender fingers across the sky like watercolor pastels.

We passed overwhelming stretches of corn fields and meadows overgrown with buckwheat. Windmills towered far off in the distance, glaring down at us like gladiators poised to strike at any minute. I'd never seen this much nature in my life. The gas stations looked like relics of a bygone time.

The drive into Fifth Street did nothing to quell my racing mind. The further we drove into the subdivision, the more my anxiety levels peaked. The road leading to our development was littered with unoccupied houses. I counted a few which had their windows boarded up with a "for sale" sign in front of them.

"Dad ..."

"Yes, son?" he said, deflated.

"Why did we move here again?"

My mom let out a groan. She had most certainly rolled her eyes.

"It was a good investment," he said cuttingly.

Uprooting all our lives and investing in a place like this directly contradicted his claim that he had "gotten over" his "gambling problem." That was what he called his addiction. A problem. Mother dearest wasn't my refuge. I probably hated that cold bitch more than him.

There was no love in this car.

We pulled into the house at noon, just before the movers arrived.

"I've gotta unload something from the trunk; you think you could hold the front door open?"

"Why, of course," she said with a shrug.

He handed the key over to her. She pinched it out of his hand as if he'd handed her a used handkerchief.

If this is what love looked like, I wanted none of it. My friends' parents had no hard edges. No obvious conflicts. They looked like they enjoyed being in each other's company. My parents' relationship was different. It was a push and pull between chaos and control. One tried to control the other, and the other responded with resentment. Rinse, repeat.

That night, I did something I'd only done when I was much younger: I wet the bed. I didn't realize this, though, until the next day. I rose with my back drenched, partly from the sweltering summer heat. Mostly from the rancid urine. Dad could smell it from the door. He stepped into the room smelling like last night's alcohol. He shot that glare at me that made my muscles cramp in my chest.

"You're a stupid little shit, you know that? Don't think I don't know what you did. You're going to sleep in it again tonight; understand?"

All I could do was nod, eyes looking down at the mess I'd made.

Life on Fifth Street was lonely. I expected our neighbors to descend on us with warm welcomes and baked treats ... despite obvious visual evidence indicating this likely wouldn't be the case. Call it the naivete of a dumb kid whose parents let him watch too much TV.

I'd started concocting scenarios of imaginary neighbors. A single mom named Carol whose son was off serving in Afghanistan, a man whose dream it was to open up a deli, and a friendly couple who came over to invite my parents to their paper anniversary.

Most of my life was spent with parents who didn't have many friends either. I assumed that if they made friends, they'd be nicer.

~

In the middle of one of my daydreams, I remember having heard a faint conversation. Mom was standing by the door; her hands animatedly gesticulated, mirroring the tone of her sing-song voice.

In front of her stood a couple that looked to be in their late thirties. They smiled. They breathed. They weren't a figment of my imagination; they were real.

The man's eyes met mine, and my entire body locked up.

"Hey there, sport," the man said.

My tongue went bone dry in my mouth.

"Harry, I think a cat's got this poor young boy's tongue."

A moment passed, and footsteps tapped behind me.

"Good afternoon," Dad said, standing next to me with his arms crossed.

"How do you do?" Mr. Jennings responded, extending a hand to him.

Mrs. Jennings handed Mom a pie tray as they exchanged the usual Hallmark pleasantries. Ever so slowly, their words began to make sense. My toehold on reality inched back in, little by little.

"Your son looks like he'd get along with our little Joseph. Perhaps he'd like to meet him. How does that sound, huh? Sorry." Mrs. Jennings let out an embarrassed chuckle. "I don't think I've learned your name?"

"This guy, I swear," Dad said, shaking his head. "Go on now, boy, don't be rude."

I mentally grasped for words, yet nothing came. I looked up and met Dad's intense glare. If I didn't spit something out then, I'd be in big trouble.

"D-Dane ..." I muttered.

"Well, it's lovely to meet you, Dane. I'm sure Joseph would be thrilled to meet you. He's a bit older, but I'm sure you'll get along. He was so nervous to move, but this lovely cul-de-sac is a fantastic real estate investment, if I do say so myself."

There was that damned word again: *investment.*

"Well, I've got to head out now," Mom said, practically pushing past them as she tucked her stringy hair behind her head.

They were well into their conversation, and Dad still hadn't invited them in. They eventually took this as their not-so-subtle hint to leave.

"Well, nice meeting you, Forester. Feel free to swing by any time, boss."

"Likewise," is all Dad said before they left.

He walked back into the study and slammed the door behind him. The clink of ice in a glass told me he was pouring himself a fresh bourbon. It was barely noon.

Social anxiety must run in the family. It's something I saw in both my parents, and it's something that made making friends in school a daunting task. Still, the name repeated itself over and over in my head.

Joseph.

Who was he? What did he look like? Did he have many friends?

CHAPTER 3: NOW

A red dot blinks out of a crack in the wall. It's a camera recording a live feed of Joe and me dying. Somewhere, some people—who knows how many—are paying good money to watch us suffer.

Our captor calls himself The Puppetmaster. We, however, are to refer to him as Sir. Sir likes to light up after he's through with us. He doesn't take a portable ashtray with him because my stomach, thighs, and face work just fine.

The wood squeaks overhead with each concussive thud.

He is here.

Iron scrapes against the concrete as the door opens. Sir steps in, a silhouette in contrast to the dim backlight of the doorway.

He positions himself in front of his rusty scaffolding desk. His broad shoulders and brawny back swell under his thin, white tank top.

If I were to guess, I'd say he stands about six-foot-five. His face is obscured by a white mask: it's cracked in several places and sports a wide, black-lipped grin.

He has a beer belly and a thick patch of hair from his chest up to the base of his neck. His arm is almost as thick as my thigh. He wears a black leather apron.

"Did you miss me?"

He straps on his black latex gloves, opening and closing his fists to ensure his brawny hands are all nice and snug.

He tosses his briefcase onto the table.

"I come bearing gifts," he says, clicking open the briefcase. "I came across these in some junkyard and bought them just for you faggots. I hope you appreciate them."

White hot rage burns in my chest. I want to hurt him. I want to hurt him so badly, even if just with words. I want to wound him just a little.

When I ignore him, he just takes his anger out on Joe. And given Joe's current state, I can't tell how much longer he will last. Joe's body is a mosaic of cuts, gashes, bashes, burns, and bruises. His entire left foot has been amputated with a rusty saw. Sewing nails were jammed beneath all of his nail beds. The Puppetmaster has desecrated his beautiful body, has cut degrading words into him with a rusty nail. On his stomach, his ribs—fag, shit, bitch ...

Across the room, a man's decapitated head stares at us. In the far corner of the room, the wall is adorned with raw meat and entrails, plastic bags containing dismembered and dissected anatomical parts that used to be people. The walls are painted completely red.

"Vicky pissed me off today. It was her turn to sort out the taxes this month, you see. Turns out she had some brand-spankin'-new plans to go out to brunch with her rich bimbo gal friends. I've been married to this fat fucking broad for twenty-odd years! All she's done is help me realize why some cultures drown their female infants."

He scatters the contents of his briefcase on the table in front of him; the effect is that of cymbals clanging together.

"You know that new strip mall over at Don's? They've got this new fish market. Fresh stuff. I've been poppin' in now and then buying fresh trout, and damn, dead fish guts are starting to smell like your friend over there."

I don't make a sound. I don't take his bait.

"I just put in the downpayment for the new Land Rover I plan on getting next week. I need a fucking vacation. I know that the old broad is likely going to bitch and moan the whole time, but these days, I'll take what I can get."

He stops to hock out a loogie and spit in the corner.

"Fuckin' allergies."

The contrast between his nonchalance and what I've seen him do sends fractals of ice slicing through my marrow.

His eyes travel up and down my naked, damaged body. He leers at me and licks his lips, rubbing a growing bulge in his crotch. He pockets the silver lighter after lighting his cigarette and walks toward us. He then digs his gunk-caked fingernails into the yellow, oozing gashes on my thigh. I shrink backward as the sharp pain burns in sudden bursts.

"You are beautiful, you know. Such strange colors the tears of your body make."

He reaches down and gropes between my legs, gently running his hand on my dick. It doesn't harden. He reaches under me and grabs my ass, practically using one arm to hoist me up. It's like sitting on a rickety bicycle seat. He bends over and licks the entire right side of my face, from my chin to my ear, in one slick line.

I wince and try to turn away.

He responds by grabbing a fistful of my hair and forcefully yanking my head back. The pain at the base of my head screams like a knife has been forcefully wedged into my vertebrae. My scalp burns as bits of hair are torn from their follicles.

"My, my, how testy you are today. I'll tell you what, you little shit, when I'm done with you—which won't be any time soon—I'll finish you off by fucking this pretty little bruised eye socket. I'll take that hook over there and gouge out both your beautiful blue eyes and shove one in your mouth, tape your mouth shut, and shove my cock in your skull. I bet the inside of your head is nice and warm. I'll save up my load so it feels nice and special when I stab you in the chest and fuck the hole so deep my cock punches your heart."

He ends this unhinged rant by hocking a loogie at my face.

"But, for now, we're going to continue our game. The rules stand: if you lose, he dies."

He stands up and makes his way back to his table of torture devices.

CHAPTER 4: SUMMER OF 2004

The adjustment period to this suburb was a difficult one; it was far more rural than the one we'd moved from. It was hills, lakes, long, winding roads, and boarded-up houses. It was practically a ghost town. At night, it would grow curiously quiet, lacking the regular sonata of cicadas and crawdads. Walk a few blocks down and you'd find yourself in the woods. A few paces into the woods sat a placid lake I had yet to explore.

I could have left home and not come back until the next day, and my parents would have just assumed I was in my room. I was a roommate they didn't know too well who they subsidized with money, not time. *I'm here*, I wanted to say. These words comforted me. I said them aloud to myself when I was alone. *Here I am, everyone, brought back to Earth.* I feared that a furious gust of wind would blow me away and make me disappear forever. The thought of vanishing soothed me.

I thought to ask Dad about it, but he hated to argue. How he treated his lawn would be a point of contention. When you so much as questioned him, you'd be dismissed. He only cared to have conversations he was interested in for the sole purpose of backing you into a corner only to demonstrate how right he was. This treatment wasn't limited to me; the old bitch got the brunt of it. When she talked back, *I* got whipped with a belt because he couldn't put his hands on her ... even though I know she wished he had. After all, that would've given her an excuse to leave him and his endless fucking *investments* and *problems*.

He only whipped me when he was drunk. When he was sober, he'd punish me by assigning a tremendous amount of chores that no human could do in a day, like cutting the grass and cleaning the entire house. I had this recurring daydream where I died and the tree outside died with me. Maybe everyone secretly just wants to end it all no matter how painful the method of doing so may be ... with certainty comes comfort.

My parents and I had drastically different schedules, so I had to get breakfast for myself. I wasn't allowed to use the stove because Mom said my "dumbass will find a way to burn the entire fucking house down."

So, I had to settle for cereal. The milk had gone sour that day, so I had to use water. The fruity cereal dyed the water a sickening shade of violet. Food coloring and sugar were on my morning menu. My molars were in an intermittent state of dull aching—I didn't waste time wondering where that came from. Telling them about this would be a foolproof path to a lecture on "how much better" I had it than other kids.

After breakfast, I walked out the front door, stepping into the day's heat. I lapped up the sun like it was liquid gold. Small joys. The dried leaves crackled under my shoes like potato chips. Much as my parents claimed to love the place, they didn't seem to give two shits about what the lawn looked like to the rest of the neighborhood.

I walked past a couple of blocks in a quest for human life, determined to rid myself of the feeling of being the lone protagonist of a dystopian tale. Dad never noticed what I had taken from his glove compartment. I, of course, had to fight off the monsters concealed behind the trees. They had red eyes and sharp claws, and they'd gut me if I wasn't ready.

I leaned against the bark of a tree, letting the sun drape on my forehead like golden liquid. My attention was caught by a pack of rowdy kids riding past me on their bikes. They laughed and shoved at one another as they parked on the side of the road. They joined in with two other boys sitting by the curb with a stereo, Bon Jovi's "Livin' on a Prayer" blasting on the speakers.

"What do you mean you're too fucking scared? How are we supposed to go ghost hunting at night if you can't even do it while the sun's out?"

"I figured we could all go together, then—"

"Bullshit. You're just fuckin' scared."

I noticed the bigger of the boys see me; an idea flashed on his face. Sensing unwanted attention coming my way, I put my head down and turned to walk away.

I'd always been too shy to approach other kids. I never wanted to impose; I'd been raised to feel unwelcome. I was afraid that if I went up to them, they'd think I was presumptuous or rude. Sometimes it's better to go through nothing instead of getting your hopes up only for it all to go to shit.

"Hey, dude, what's up? How's it going? You got a minute?" the kid asked, addressing me.

I stepped past them, increasing my steps and pretending I didn't hear anything. I unwittingly caught the glance of one guy. He pressed his palms to the nearby tree, cornering me.

Fuck.

"Hey, man, I'm talking to you. Are you trying to be an asshole or something?"

"H-hey," I said quietly.

He nudged the girl next to him, and then a couple more of them glared at me.

What the hell did I do?

"So, here's the deal," the kid continued. "We live nearby, and we plan on going ghost hunting in the woods tonight. We're very excited with it being summer and all; I'm sure you can tell. We can stay up later at night. We're thinking you'd be a cool new friend and sample the woods for us. Tell us if it's safe?" The kid flashed me the grin of a used car salesman. "So, you gonna do it?"

I muscled my jaw into a polite smile and shook my head. I wasn't the type to smile, ever. Doing so made me feel icky and embarrassed. I had always thought my smile was repulsive, that showing it to people made them cringe.

"What's that supposed to mean?"

"No."

"No?" The kid smirked, looking back at his gang and then back to me. "You're fucking kidding, right?"

"Hey, loser! Where did all your friends go?" one of them yelled.

The rest laughed in unison.

With my hand still raised, I flipped them the bird. Fuck those fat piss-drinking fucks.

I'd been in a couple of fights. One was in the first grade, the other was last year when another kid tried to steal my lunch money. That encounter had gone so wrong I nearly got kicked out of school. My parents were furious. Since then, I'd vowed to avoid any future conflict. Still, bullshit had a way of finding me. It was as if being an asshole was contagious.

"You've got some balls, faggit."

The tall kid shoved me backward. I fell, and my wrist scraped against the hot gravel.

"I'm sorry," I said, my voice laced with anxiety.

"What, not so tough now, huh? You retarded fag. Go back home and jerk it to gay porn; we all know you do, bro."

I hobbled back to my feet. Before I could process what just happened, he pushed me back into a tree. The jutting tree bark stabbed into my back through my thin shirt. My stomach sank. I'd tried so hard to keep to myself, and now this. The tall kid stepped closer, going full tilt. I was cornered.

I had nowhere else to go. I reached into my pocket and found the metal handle. I squeezed it with one hand and made a fist with the other. A wave of furious anger swelled inside me. The brute inched closer.

"You are a loser freak, aren't you?

Before he could say another fucking word, my dad's switchblade was jammed against his neck. I held it up to his face, then pressed it back down to his jugular. I remembered the kid who tried to snatch my lunch money. I'd punched him so hard in the face that the entire top of his uniform was stained red. If this guy called me a faggot one more time, he was going to find out real quick.

"Say that again?" I hissed.

He stood there, frozen.

"Hey, man, we were just playing; lighten up."

Really?

"Let him go, you freakshow!" one girl yelled.

I pulled the knife back from his throat, placating them. Then I raised the knife over my head so fast that one of the other girls screamed. I flung my arm down, stopping the blade right in front of his eye. He violently gasped. I soaked in the blanched faces of his companions.

"Leave me. The fuck. Alone," I said through gritted teeth.

He hastily nodded and ran back to his cabal of fuckheads. A dark patch stained his crotch and ran down his legs.

He hopped on his bike and took off; the rest followed suit with haste. If I could make a list of one hundred things that scared me, the top spot would go to other people. I may not have been as tall and sturdy as most boys my age, but weapons were a fantastic equalizer.

I spent the next few days by the shallow lake. I spotted those kids in the vicinity several times, but none of them dared come near me. I guessed they weren't complete fucktards. I walked to the edge of the lake and sat down on a moss-caked log. The lake was as tranquil as a mirror's surface; it reflected billowing migrant clouds drifting across the salmon twilight. Resting next to me was a bucket of crayfish.

I liked to watch them squirm and wriggle on top of one another to determine who the alpha was. In the far-off distance, a couple of those boys spoke in what Dad referred to as *locker room talk*. I recalled the awkwardness of having to share a communal bathroom with guys my age. The conversations I'd had to hear as a result of being relegated to spaces with older boys were vile. The way they spoke about girls, the way they talked about which free porn sites had the "hottest babes to bust a fat load to." I learned you could search for pretty much anything: "underage twins suck their stepdad's cock," "dyke forced to try cock for the first time and cries," and "lesbian anal peg party."

When I'd asked my mom about it, she had brushed me off and told me that those boys were "going through a phase." I wondered when I'd go through this phase. I wondered why I wasn't as enthusiastic about girls, breasts, or, "squirting bitch taking it raw." I had this intense inkling that something in me was *wrong*.

Every time I heard one of those boys speak, my first instinct was to look for my dad's shotgun and blow my fucking brains out. A hobby of mine—indulgent afternoon daydreaming of suicide. My old man's shotgun between my lips like a cock, a bang, a violent jerk, blood and brain matter wetting grass beneath me.

"Have you named those crabs?" a boy said, startling me out of my macabre reverie.

Standing next to me was the most beautiful person I'd ever seen. A figure of a young boy with rays of buttery, golden light lighting up half his face; the hues of waning sunlight suited his luminous tan.

Wait, crabs?

My mind then went to the bucket next to me—I'd planned on releasing the crayfish before I headed home. He wasn't one of the assholes I met the other day, which likely made him the Jennings kid. I hadn't expected to make any friends, but I did have stupid hope.

"C-crabs?" I said.

"Yeah, those things in there. They're crabs." He scratched the back of his head during a pregnant pause. "Aren't they?"

"N-no, actually ... they're crayfish. Here, look." I picked up the bucket and handed it over to him. "Crabs live in the ocean, you know ... salt water. Have you ever been to a beach?"

"Nah, my parents hate the sun. I've always wanted to go, though," he said, dragging his feet along the sodden earth.

He spoke with a soft, lilting tone. One that didn't have much confidence in it. His voice shook a bit, like he was supremely shy. He was older than me, likely in middle school, definitely in the double-digits. I was still in the third grade.

"So, what are you doing back here?" I asked.

"Oh yeah, my parents and I just moved in a couple of weeks ago. They said I needed to go out more ... Summer is the time for making friends and stuff. They said I could have an extra hour on the PlayStation if I made a friend, and an extra hour on top of that if I got a friend—or friends—to come over to the house.

"What's a PlayStation?"

"You're kidding, right?

"N-no?"

"Oh, man, it's this thing ... like, have you ever been to an arcade?"

"That place in the mall with the fighting games you need to stick a coin in? And then you choose your fighter?"

"Yeah! So with a PlayStation, you can play some of those games at your place, for free, for as long as you want."

Free arcade games and friendship? Sign me the fuck up.

"You've gotta show me! What games do you have?"

"Oh, I've got *Tekken*, *Street Fighter*, *Power Rangers Turbo* … stuff like that. Wanna come over to the house today?"

I didn't even bother trying to stifle my pathetic grin.

"Sure."

"Awesome."

He smiled. I smiled back.

"So have you met any of the other kids?" He looked around. "I ran into a couple of them on the way out of the grocery store. My parents told me to introduce myself because they looked to be my age. I was too shy, though."

"How old are you?"

"I'm twelve, turning thirteen in October. You?"

"Nine … gonna be ten in December."

"Cool. I'm Joe, by the way."

"I'm Dane."

"Cool to meet ya, Dane. So, do you know those other kids?"

"You mean those assholes and cunts?"

"Assholes and cuh-what?" he said.

"Cunts," I said, barely holding back a giggle.

We both burst out into laughter. We laughed so long we must've looked like we'd just smoked an entire bowl.

"I have *met* them. They don't like me."

"Why?"

"Because one of those chickenshit asswipes tried to scare me, so I brought this out."

I hesitated before taking out the switchblade; the last thing I wanted to do was scare off perhaps the only person willing to be my friend. If he freaked out, I could kiss the friendship and free arcade games goodbye. I said *fuck it*. He stared at the switchblade, mouth agape.

"C-cool …" was all he said.

CHAPTER 5: NOW

The Puppetmaster straightens the tripod and points the lamp at me. My eyelids sag with exhaustion as my heart thuds in my chest like a door slamming. The back of my head itches, yet as I attempt to scratch it, the cuffs dig their rusted talons into my flesh. Each breath sends a pulse of excruciating pain down my back. I clamp down on the ball gag to stifle a scream.

"Don't bother struggling. No one ever escapes. Those noodle arms will break themselves trying to pry those chains loose," he says, sharpening some tools.

I nudge Joe with my shoulder. Joe stirs and lets out a labored moan but is unable to open his swollen eyes. Repeated beatings make it look as if golf balls have been surgically implanted beneath his skin. A yellow-gray cloth is secured around his mouth. His entire body is bound by barbed wire, penetrating the flimsy barrier of flesh above his muscles. Seeing him in this state is an endurance test in and of itself. If I could just get my damn hands on one of this fucker's tools ... forceps, pliers, box cutters, hammers, meat cleavers, bladed whips, chains ...

Puppetmaster steps toward me and undoes the hook behind my head. He eases the ball gag out of my mouth and rubs my jaw. *Click!* The corners of my jaw cramp as I bring my chapped lips together.

"I'm going to want to hear you speak as we play our fun little game," he says.

He turns around and makes his way up the stairs.

"Listen to me well, Joe," I whisper.

Joe lets out a groan.

"I'm going to get us out. This sick fuck isn't going to get away with this. Just hang on a bit longer."

"Kill ... me ..." Joe rasps.

A tidal wave of despair crashes over me.

"No. Never. Joe, j-just hold on ... please, don't go. I beg you." I lean in closer to him, wanting to pull him into a hug, wanting to take his hand and hold him. But I can't, so I just lean on him. My heart is a boulder sitting on my chest.

I run through the arid scenarios in my head. How can I trick this fucker into releasing me so I can jump him? Will I have enough time to run out of the door? Find a telephone where I can call 911? Is there anything in this room I can tie him up with? Is this his house; and is there a landline upstairs I can use? Fuck ... I doubt we're still even in New York. One thing is for certain ... for me to get out of here, this man is going to have to die. One of us is going to end up being a killer, and I am not going to let it be Joe. He was a big brother to me growing up, and now I need to be here for him.

"Shh, Joe, pretend to be asleep. I think he's coming back."

After a brief shuffling of footsteps, the metal grates against the concrete. The Puppetmaster materializes in my peripheral vision, holding the head of a woman. She stares right at me with her single brown eye. The other one is sewn shut, with tar-like fluid seeping down from the lid. Her ratty hair is caked with dust and grime. She's on all-fours. Her forearms and shins have been amputated; her mouth is sewn shut.

She is pregnant.

He drags her by the hair as she crawls, struggling to meet his pace. He then turns to me, his mask flashing that ear-to-ear smile.

"Allow me to introduce you two. I don't know her name, but I call her Piper. I named her after my mother, you see. They had the same color of eyes—I mean, eye." He lets out a loud guffaw, throwing his head back, practically howling at his joke.

"She's been fun. She's been here a while, though. I should've snuffed this bitch weeks ago, but Sadie loves her. You see, I told Sadie I'd get her a doll. You've gotta admit, amputees make fantastic toys."

She looks up at me. Her eye is lifeless.

"My mom caught me jerking off to this porno once. Well, I dunno if I'd call it a porno. Basically, she stormed out and pretended she'd seen nothing. I was smacking it to this VHS a classmate of mine got me. The Asian bitch in it was pregnant, you see, and this one guy was holding her down. She wasn't gagged, so I could hear all her delicious screams. Those fucking howls she was making, phew-wee! I love it when you can't tell the difference between a bitch cumming and a bitch getting knifed in her pussy. Fuck, I'm getting hard just thinking of it. Her legs were wide open. Someone had attached this wire to her clit to electrocute her. I was pumping so fast and hard ... I damn near almost nutted when the man with the tattoos tore open her belly with his bare hands and ripped that sack of flesh out of her gut with that hook. But just as I was about to bust, mommy dearest came in. She shut the door and apologized. I never forgave her for interrupting that moment, for ruining the first time I ever came to the sight of something better than the most hardcore porn I'd seen. We had no locks on our doors ... grew up in a very strict religious house where privacy was in short supply."

He cracks his neck and looks at Piper.

"Anyway, I've always wanted to try a fetus. May I have yours?"

She doesn't react. She's completely out of it.

"I'm just gonna finish up with her before I get to you, boy." He laughs again.

My breath catches in my throat as his foot collides with her pregnant belly. Under normal circumstances, she'd belt out like a banshee, yet she remains sedate. He likely doped her up on something. She lands on her back, eyes glazed over like she's in a state of religious ecstasy. He pries open her leg stumps, exposing her to the camera. The flesh of her labia is rife with dead, gangrenous tissue.

He takes a syringe and dips the needle into a container of bleach. Once the barrel is filled, he slides the needle down to the hub into her pregnant belly and presses down on the plunger. She writhes as her tongue darts in and out of her toothless maw to lick dribbling bits of discharge from her nostril.

Almost instantly, yellow millipedes of pus wriggle out from between her thighs. He unzips his pants and wraps his hands around her neck as he slides his erection into her. He begins to pump into her as blood and yellow pus spume out of her cunt like bubbles popping in tree sap. He squeezes his grip on her neck as he thumps his bare pelvis back and forth into her. Her face rouges as he slams into her down to the hilt; he squeezes her neck so hard that her bones snap like walnuts breaking.

While he's inside her, he unsheathes a large hunting knife. He digs the tip of the knife into her left breast. She tries to shriek, but all that comes out is a labored gasp. He begins to cut wedges into the nipple like a chef preparing cold cuts. He cores out her nipple and peels the skin back from the fat and flesh beneath. He then pulls out of her, waddles up to his knees, and slides the end of his cock into the fatty crevice. A mix of growls and groans emanates from under his mask. He then gets to his feet and stomps so hard on her pregnant belly that gruelly clumps of pulverized meat fizz and sputter from her cunt.

My throat constricts as acid upchuck belches out of me, into the tub. I hack and gag; burning tears well up in the corners of my eyes. The smell of decay and blood is overpowering. As my blurry vision comes back into focus, all I'm met with is the Puppetmaster's smile and dark orbs for eyes. It's like those onyx pits can sense and absorb my fear. Throughout all of this, his cock remains erect.

"Enjoy that? Before I get to you, I'm gonna need a drink. If you couldn't already tell, we make the best fetish porn in this studio. This stuff was tame. Most of

Novak's clients love watching humiliation, high impact beatings, shit, piss, bestiality ... Best we can do with this cunt is probably a time-lapse clip of her corpse decomposing."

He unearths a flask from the pocket of his apron.

"Nothing like some good old Jack after a hard day's work, eh, Fido? That's what Novak calls you, right? Fido. Ya like it?"

He grabs a chair by its frame and pulls it up next to me. The grating of the metal on the granite floor stings like nails on a chalkboard. Sitting down, he casually scrolls through his phone. The light from the screen lights up his face.

"Sorry, I'll get back to you in a jiffy—am just checking emails. Fuck. The damn contractor says he won't be able to make it tomorrow. Can't let him reschedule for the next day because I promised the old lady I'd take her out to dinner. It's our anniversary tonight."

The thought that he lives a normal life outside of *all this* makes me fucking sick. Despite this, nausea and drowsiness weigh on me as my eyes slacken, searching for any semblance of rest. A cold, sharp object gently brushes against my face, and I jolt backward with a start. He holds a large serrated blade mere inches from my face.

"Don't sleep when I am talking to you."

"Fuck you, and fuck the mother that shat you out."

"There he is! There's feisty Fido."

"So you're gonna kill me, huh? You're gonna fuck me to death, you're gonna kill Joe, and then what? What the fuck is Novak getting out of this?"

"He doesn't like it when his pets threaten to leave. Also, I don't care who you are; this is never not fun."

"Nothing you do to me is gonna hurt me. Kill me, just let this guy go, man. I'll do whatever those sick fucks watching want."

He leans in closer to me. "You play by my rules, got that? And if you don't play nice, I'm gonna hurt him. And if he dies, that's gonna be on you."

A bulb of unease expands in my chest as I look into the endless black pools where his eyes should be.

He continues. "You've got a hefty pair of balls; I'll give ya that. Let me remind you that I've got a knife pointed right in your face. One thrust forward and I'll puncture your pretty blue eye. Has skull-fucking ever been one of your weird kinks? I'd love nothing more than to bust a nut in that pretty little head of yours."

My eyes burn. The back of my neck throbs like it has been injected with cold gas from being propped up in this awkward position for far too long. I cry—or, at least, I think I am crying. My sobs scrape in my throat, which has all the moisture of burnt toast. But my mind retaliates against me as I try to take in a deep breath because of the massive lesion of despair inside my chest.

"Look, I can't do anything to you until Sadie gets here, so this first game is going to be easy."

He presses the serrated edge of the knife right below the crook of Joe's jaw, right where his pulse rises and falls against it.

"You and I are gonna watch a movie. If you happen to look away for just a second, I'll cut something off him." He nudges his head toward Joe. "The clients won't mind if he's missing an ear. Or a toe. Or a finger. Or his balls. Heck, if I carve his balls out, they might even like it more—I'll fuck him in the bloody hole. I'm sure it'll feel way better than a wet cunt."

My body locks up. I want to crack every bone in my body just to loosen things up. My teeth gnash so tight my jaw begins to cramp.

He scrolls through his phone—faster now—and stops to look at me.

"Here's what my idea of fun looks like; hey that's me! That mask look familiar? Ah, and that over there, that's Sadie in the mask with the bunny ears and the strap-on dildo. Cute, ain't she?"

The video begins.

Darkness.

"All right. First round. You're gonna watch this movie all the way through. It's directed by yours truly. I'm sure you'll notice a very familiar cameo."

The grainy footage looks like it's coming from a vintage VHS tape. Slats of light like ultra-slim perpendicular beams cut across a darkened wall. The camera inches closer to the brightness as the image comes into focus. A pregnant woman walks around a kitchen alone, setting down bags of groceries and placing their contents on the counter. She goes about this task with an air of complete obliviousness.

Cut.

The camera lurches down a dark hallway. Its quality is grainy—an old fluorescent blue hue superimposed with erratic fuzz. At the end of the hall is a door held slightly ajar. A closeup shot of the door sees that same woman naked, towel-drying her hair. She brushes her damp hair and slips on a pair of pink lace underwear. Behind her, from the bathroom mirror, is a figure. The figure just stands there. Out of sheer impulse, I nearly yelled out in terror, begging the woman to turn around. Run down the stairs. Yell out the window for the neighbors—anything! She doesn't. She just stands, combing her hair as she stares into the mirror. She doesn't sense it as the figure in the bathroom approaches her.

"Piper," the person holding the camera says.

Piper, or whoever this woman is, snaps toward the camera with a look of daggers.

It's her. It's the woman who was just killed.

I retch as acidic bile barrels up my throat. I nearly look away, then remember what he promised to do to Joe if I did.

Piper stands there, catatonic. Her fight-slash-flight response seems to have checked out; she's chosen to *freeze*. The cameraperson approaches her slowly. From the bottom right of the camera, a hand with a gun emerges, pointing straight at her pregnant belly. Her face crumples up as she starts to sob. She holds her hands up in meek surrender. Her pale, translucent skin pinkens as her once serene disposition shatters. She then clutches her hands together in a sort of prayer, begging to be spared, begging the heavens for help. Before she can utter a prayer, a figure behind her forcefully shoves a wad of cloth over her mouth. Her entire body loosens as she is rendered completely sedated.

Cut.

A dank basement. There are a couple of light bulbs dangling from the ceiling. It's this basement. The lights in the basement are stained blood-red. The Puppetmaster's mask comes into focus as he sets up the camera angle. Everything is bathed in a filter of deep red.

Cut.

Piper is propped up in front of the camera. She is tied to a chair. Her mouth is duct taped and bound so tight a rash has formed on her cheeks. Two people stand on either side of her. Her hair is disheveled. She is naked. Her hands are shackled behind her, and her spread feet are nailed to two heavy-looking, wooden blocks. She's wearing some sort of leather S&M dog collar. Streaks of black mascara run down her red face from her bloodshot eyes. On one side stands a man with a plague mask. Next to him is a woman in a leather dog mask wearing a strap-on dildo. They're both naked. The man strokes himself as the woman lubes up the dildo with some sort of black liquid.

The man hooks clamps to Piper's nipples as the masked woman fills up a leather glove with coins. Piper screams into the tape as even more black eyeliner drips down her face onto her breasts. Sadie grabs the girl's hair, pulls back her hand, and wallops her in the cheek with the coin-filled glove. Piper's head snaps to the side as blood and mucus bubble from her cracked nose. Her muffled screams fight against the tape.

The man gets on his knees and pries her cunt open with his fingers and licks her hairy center. She resists and screams some more, only to be struck once again by Sadie, this time three consecutive blows to her right breast. The man continues to stimulate her as her head hangs low, and blood falls onto his head.

Cut.

Sadie grabs Piper's collar and yanks her neck up, facing her head to the camera. Her delirious eyes are framed by a swollen face painted deep purple and crimson. Piper gags as Sadie yanks the collar up. The man wrestles Piper to the ground and props her up onto all-fours as Sadie parts her legs. Sadie rams her dildo into her asshole. She responds with a helpless, garbled cry. The man strokes himself as Sadie annihilates her anal cavity. The man leans in and spits on her face as he pumps himself ferociously. He grabs her by the throat and squeezes, choking her as he tugs his cock so hard and fast the head starts to turn purple.

In my peripheral vision, the Puppetmaster begins to rub on his crotch. A bulge conspicuously forms.

Cut.

The man pulverizes her mouth with a hammer. When he's done, he hoists her up on this suspension device that looks like a primitive sex swing. Teeth and gooey liquid spill out of her slackened jaw. His gore-stained cock sticks out of a tuft of tangled pubic hair before it disappears into her mangled mouth. With nearly all her teeth missing, there's nothing she can do to resist. He bucks into her so hard she retches, and vomit ejaculates all over his cock. This doesn't deter him one bit.

"Fuck, it's so nice and warm," he rasps, quickening his pace.

Behind Piper, Sadie holds the lubricated dildo up and sinks it into the sphincter of her asshole, then buries the large toy completely inside with a slam. She's being completely spit-roasted. Sadie pumps into her so hard that humiliating farting sounds belch out of her asshole.

Cut.

The camera rests on the woman's vacant expression.

"Keep. Fucking. Watching ..."

Cut.

Sadie grabs Piper by the hair and yanks her head back as her back arches. The man whispers to Sadie an order, and she yanks the shit-stained dildo out of Piper's rectum. The man sticks the forceps between her lips, prying her bleeding mouth open. Sadie then grabs the back of her head and rams the crap-stained dildo down her throat, forcing her to swallow the filth. All she does is gag and puke again.

The man laughs as Sadie gets on her knees and begins to fellate him. He forces his cock into her mouth so hard her head bucks backward and she vomits on the floor. Before she can take a breath, the man rams his cock into her mouth once again. Sadie begins to tear up, though her eyes beam in absolute jubilation. Thrust, squeeze, thrust, squeeze ...

A distinct rubbing noise to my side shows me that Sir is masturbating right next to my head. His hand moves up and down in tandem with his thrusts into the head of Sadie on the screen, focusing on this poor woman's tortured face. He stands, positioning himself in front of me, sinking one of his feet into the tub of blood half-submerging Joe and I. The purple, crusted head of his cock looks me right in the face as he aggressively pumps himself. The slapping sound echoes throughout the whole room.

"I've put my knife away, but the same rule stands. Do ... not ... look away," he says, panting in between words.

His nut is timed perfectly with Sadie's scream. Ribbons of hot pearlescent sludge shoot out of the tip of his now dark-red, crooked prick. It lands on my face ... my mouth, my eyes. I violently thrash, trying to get it off me.

"Did you like tasting your master's load, you little slut? I have it on my phone because I like to tug it to my art. I wouldn't call it work, though. I'd do this all for free. I enjoy it. What's that saying about doing something you love and not ever having to work a day in your life? Anyway—that's me. I fuckin' love my life."

He swats me, and I skid back, shrinking into the tub. If I wasn't tied up, I'd lunge at him, my fist up, rageful as I always got when I was about to start a fight. Go for the chin, then the nose. Make him bleed, crack his teeth, smack that stupid jackwit mask off his face, and tear his eyes out.

Instead, he grabs me by the neck and says, in the soothing tone of a talk-show host, "Did you like that, you little slut?"

All I can do is nod helplessly, trying to placate him. That question takes me back to a time in my life I vowed to never return to. My reaction to it is instinctive. It takes me back to—

"Good. That, ladies and gents, is Snuff-23. Piper was twenty-three, and that's how we name these movies. You, on the other hand ... I don't know how old you are, but you don't look a day over seventeen. I suppose we're gonna call your movie Snuff-17."

He swipes a hand through his bangs.

"The more you cooperate, the easier this will be. Yes, I'll have to carve your flesh, make some new holes, and fuck those open gashes, but think about how much joy that brings Sadie and me! They like it when I play with my food. If I could have it my way, I'd take that scalpel, carefully slice you open, and fuck your innards while you watch. Novak said our client said he loves the way you hurt yourself on The Red Den."

What the hell?

"He says your whole schtick is inflicting pain on yourself. Granted, a lot of it is fake, and it's nothing compared to what I am going to do to you ... And yes, you will be kept alive as long as possible."

He turns to me, his mask perpetually contorted in a psychotic grin. He has a meat cleaver in one hand and a hook in the other.

"Now, shall we begin?"

CHAPTER 6: SUMMER OF 2004

Mr. Jennings insisted that Joe teach me how to fish. We sidled through weeks, carrying our poles toward the lake. Fish bones and used lures littered the edge of the bank. A breeze fluttered through the overhead leaves and circled the water's edge like an invisible tether. The scent of honeydew and the rustling of nature reminded me of a faint pattering of applause.

Joe grunted and extracted a bass lure from the tackle box.

"Do you know what you're doing?" I asked.

"Nope."

"So, why are we fishing, again?"

"Dane, do you want more time on the PlayStation or not?"

"And this is the *only* way we're gonna get it?"

"Yup."

"Fuck."

A shy giggle escaped past Joe's lips.

"Okay, so was it an extra thirty minutes for a carp and an extra hour for a largemouth bass?" I ask.

"I'm pretty sure it was the other way around. Do we get anything for catfish?"

"Gross. I hate catfish."

"Hey, it's still a fish."

"Maybe your dad likes them."

"Gross. The librarian at my old school looked like a catfish."

"Maybe Mr. Jennings thought she was hot."

"Yuck!"

"Maybe he wanted to see her boobies."

"Eww! Okay, stop!" Joe said, sticking his tongue out as if he was gagging.

Joe held the lure toward the sunlight. It looked like a ladybug with yellow feathers jutting out of its ass. He pinched it, hard, as if it was a live insect that was desperate to fly away lest it end up becoming bass chow. The warm sun bathed us in melted butter. I looked up and took in a deep breath. The confectionary Kansas air smelled like balmy flower essence in the thick of summer.

Joe went first to show me how it was done. I'd never gone fishing before—for some reason, I assumed it was going to be exciting. I was under the impression we would have buckets full of bass and endless PlayStation time. Instead, we spent what felt like the entire runtime of a *Lord of the Rings* movie staring at the bobber as it uneventfully floated in the center of the pond.

Nothing.

Joe tugged it in slowly, only for it to peek out of the water without any catch. Frustrated, I sat down and stared at the placid surface of the water. It reflected the endless azure sky and the isles of cattails across from us.

After a few minutes, Joe lost patience and turned to me.

"This sucks."

"Yeah," I scoffed, "I wish we'd just played hide and seek or something."

"Wanna see that magic trick I told you about instead?" Joe said.

"The flamethrower?"

"Yup."

"There's no way that's gonna work."

"Have a little faith, will ya?"

We moved to a clearing far into the bushel of trees that led to the pond. Joe situated a candle on the tree stump and lit the wick with a match. This place was where some of the residents used to have target practice. It was Monday, and most of the tradesmen who lived in the nearby trailer parks were off doing whatever odd jobs they could find. We had the whole place to ourselves.

"Have faith in what? You said you'd bring a flame thrower. You said it would be just like one of those Rambo movies. What the fuck is this?"

"Stand back."

He took a can of hairspray out of his rucksack and gave it a good shake. Positioning the can a few feet away from the lit candle, he pressed down on the top of the can. The transparent spray morphed into a massive plume of flames that feathered about six feet long. I stared at it as the fire quickly dissipated into thin air.

"Woah."

"Right? You can go pick up that slingshot, shoot a dove down, and eat it now."

"Fuck off."

He laughed, and so did I. He handed the can over to me, and I gave it a couple of sprays, testing the fire to see how large it would grow. The thrill of experiencing something new, something magical, and feeling it next to who was perhaps my favorite person in the entire world meant everything to me. The guilt that I could be the happiest boy in the world crept in. Before I could dwell on it any longer, Joe tapped me.

"Wanna swim?"

I paused for a moment, too shy to tell him that I didn't know how to swim. I'd only known this kid for a few days, and he was already going to think I was a fucking loser. I certainly didn't plan to lose my only shot at a friend to assholes and cunts, so I lied. This crossed a line—lying to someone you just met, who you've developed a great affinity for.

"I find the water to be a bit cold, but you go ahead. I'll just go catch some more crayfish."

"All right, suit yourself."

He took off his shirt, and I couldn't help but gawk. On land, he looked fragile; in the water, he was magnificent. A creature ordained to impress, cursed to have to walk on dry land. His body thrived in the lake; his weaknesses looked strong. He was in his element, and the effect was alchemy. His form was excellent, graceful even—not that I knew anything about swimming, but he certainly looked like he knew what he was doing.

I eventually came clean about my nonexistent swimming prowess. He didn't judge me; he just smiled and said he'd show me how. I wasn't good at first—I didn't think I'd ever be—but he was as patient as I was eager. He showed me how to stay afloat, lifting me toward the surface of the water and telling me to allow my head to lean back like it was a late-stage baptism. He then demonstrated how to kick and paddle. I came to love the feel of cool water against my skin.

Out here, with Joe, the lake washed away all my sadness. It was as if the great radiance of the sky granted me reprieve from my doubts and anguish. When I sat next to Joe, I had the feeling I could say anything to him. Any confession, no matter how shameful, would be answered with kindness and cheerful understanding.

"Joe, what if I fall into the deep end? What if I drown?"

"You won't fall. I'll be here to hold you back."

It was the most fun I'd ever had. I was still afraid to swim in the center of the lake because I'd always had this irrational fear of water so deep you couldn't see the surface. In return, I taught him how to catch crayfish.

Out here, where the wind cut the water's surface, I was warmed by the thought of this new and budding friendship. Whenever I thought of him, I felt my face grow smooth—like I was lost in a dream that could stay with me all day.

Video games were also a staple of that summer.

"I think I like *Tekken* more," I said.

"Why?"

"Because the characters feel more real. They don't have these weird superpowers and energy bolts that you shoot out of your hand that jerks like to spam."

"Are you calling me a jerk?" He nudged me playfully.

"Depends. Are you admitting now, once and for all, that you spam those stupid power blasts?"

"Never."

"Joseph Jennings."

"I admit to no such thing."

"Okay, let's play a round now. You be Ryu, and I'll count how many fucking Hadou-whatevers you use in one round."

"Hey, that's fucking unfair. Also, they're called Hadoukens."

Hearing Mister Conscientious cuss was always hilarious. My parents didn't care as long as I never directed any of those *bad words* at them. Sometimes I wish there'd been someone to tell me there were certain things you shouldn't do. Joe was swearing a lot now because he said he'd never sworn before and hearing me say it sounded *cool*. Whenever he cussed, he'd laugh at himself. This made me laugh, which made us both look like a couple of idiots. I wouldn't have had it any other way.

"Hey, thanks," is all I said.

"For?"

"Inviting me to your house?"

"Hey, are you okay?"

"Yeah, I guess it's just that I've never really had any good friends. I've always been a loner. I just never fit in. Don't laugh."

"I think you're ... you know."

"What?" I said.

"Interesting."

Interesting? I'll take it.

I smiled back.

"*Street Fighter*. Now. If you can manage to beat without spamming, you can pick what we play next," I said.

"How do I know if I'm spamming?"

"More than five Hadoukens is considered spamming."

"You're on."

CHAPTER 7: NOW

"Joe, Joe! Wake up. Are you still there?"

"Y-yeah," he murmurs.

I've since taken the brunt of the punishment, so I don't know how much more I can endure. For the first round of the game, Sir wanted to see if I'd get knocked out if he hit me with the coin glove. I wasn't, thus Joe was spared. It feels like a handful of needles has been shoved into my right cheek. He fastened my wrists with metal strands that whittle away at my flesh. My lungs ache, and my eyes are strained with tears. A crusty trail of dried snot (or blood?) is stuck just above my shuddering upper lip.

"Joe, stay with me. When did you last eat?"

He doesn't respond.

It's like he can't remember anything; he's completely out of it. I am drenched in sweat; the humidity in this blood-stained room is not good for these untreated wounds. The room is as hot as a car that's been left out in the sun.

"I ..." he says.

"Joe?"

"I ..."

"What is it, man? What's the matter, hey ..."

I lean in closer, nudging him. He rests his forehead on my shoulder, and I feel a single warm tear land on me. It takes everything in me to not completely lose it. I can't afford to show any weakness, and I can't let Joe lose whatever hope he may still have.

"I want to go home, Dane ..." he rasps from swollen lips.

The last of my strength finally dissipates. Burning tears well in the corner of my eye, the last of my body's moisture being expelled. So many tears follow. I blow a payload of snot out onto my chest to allow breathing. The sound of his voice, the way his head looks disfigured—I think this fucker might have cracked his skull or fractured his jaw. He strains to say the few words he can. When he does, they have a gravelly, forced quality to them.

No one knows where we are.

I don't know how the hell they got Joe; I don't even know if Cassandra is okay. The only person who my mind keeps racing back to, the only person who would've given a damn had I gone missing and would've tried to find me, is sitting right next to me.

"I failed, Joe. I'm sorry." I continue to cry as these words pour out of me.

"Not ... your ... fault ... I—" His head slouches down, and he starts to snore.

Nice and easy, Joe. Rest up.

If he doesn't get any medical attention soon, he's done for.

I push the thought from my head. No. He will get out of here. He will survive. There is no world where Joe doesn't exist. The thought is inconceivable.

He mumbles something else, but it hardly even meets the standard of incoherent babbling. His speech is an uneven pattern of spit bubbles and quivering lips that form indistinguishable vowel sounds that bleed into one another.

"Stop, Joe. I hear ya. Rest up, come on, try and take a nap on my shoulder."

Then, he stands. Suddenly, he's unchained. Suddenly, he's completely healed. He's smiling. He's beaming at me with those beautiful brown eyes. He smiles at me and takes my hand.

"Come now, Dane ... let's go down to the lake with the crabs."

His smile is a picture, a smile that makes you feel like you're the only person that's ever mattered in the history of the universe. A smile so innocent, you'd know that this pure, beautiful man was raised in an unconditionally loving home. You'd know he was the kind of person who strived to take that love and show it to as many people as possible. At that moment, the subject of that smile was me—the subject and the object: the sum total of everything that could make him happy is how I feel as I gaze into those compassionate eyes. The warmth of his soft, uncalloused palm is a home. Home is where this man's smile is. The only person I've ever loved.

"Come on, Dane. The lake is right there! Then we can make a map of the entire forest and sell it for a billion dollars and use that money to buy the world's biggest TV. Our fighting game characters will look like giants!" he says.

And then the warmth of the bright golden sun rests on my skin. The view is infused with air so clean you can smell the natural oils on the weeds and flowers. The sound of water flowing in the distance is iridescent.

I'm outside.

Behind Joe is the lake. The lake he taught me how to swim in. The lake where I teased him about the *crabs* that were actually *crayfish*. We're back in that summer ... we're—

CHAPTER 8: SUMMER OF 2004

—sitting by the playground, playing tic-tac-toe in the sand. We never formally decided to spend the summer together. I was usually by the creek every day after lunch up to the early afternoon. Whenever he needed me, he knew where to find me. He'd take extra snacks from his pantry to the creek because he was amused at how my eyes would light up whenever I was presented with such treats as if I'd only tried Twinkies and corndogs for the first time—which I had. When he first held the corndog out to me, I looked at him, confused, because I thought it was going to be corn. He chuckled and snorted. He didn't call me an idiot, though. He never called me anything derogatory; he was just nice.

Joe found it odd that I didn't have to ask my parents for permission to visit his house. I sort of just brushed it off because I didn't feel like telling him what my piss-poor home situation was like.

He introduced me—or reintroduced me—to Mr. Jennings, a Social Studies teacher at the school we were going to attend in the fall. He taught high school, thankfully, so neither of us would end up in his class. Joe's dad smiled a lot and liked to tell jokes like he had managed to preserve a part of his childhood after all these years. I couldn't help but compare him to my father, the old grouch who only seemed to care about what the old bitch made for dinner. Usually, they ordered takeout: pizza, Chinese food, or chicken wings with stale fries. To ensure that I didn't starve to death, we had a basket of cheap ramen noodles in the pantry.

Mr. Jennings spent the afternoon planning his lessons for the upcoming school year. Joe's mom arrived with groceries that afternoon. We had worked up a major appetite after having run around in Joe's yard all day. We helped her bring the groceries in, and Joe gave her a big hug. I wondered what that felt like. Maybe it would help if I just stopped viewing this situation through the lens of comparison; maybe a little gratitude would do the trick. I now had an older brother, a best friend I'd always wanted, and two surrogate parents I could escape to—ones who didn't exist entirely in my imagination. No, this was real. This was a moment I wish I could go back to and just live in forever.

"Did you two boys spend the whole day outside?" Mrs. Jennings asked.

"Yes, Mom, it's summer!"

"Wow. Dane, you should come over more often. When you're not here, he just plays those blasted video games all day. It's frightening how addictive these gadgets are."

A faint laugh escaped me. I couldn't remember ever having been wanted—by anyone. All of this was new to me.

"Hey, I'm making chili tonight. Would you like to stay for dinner?" Mrs. Jennings asked.

She held my gaze with rapt anticipation. She would never know this, but that small offer granted me a breath of unsalted air I thought I'd never have. She'd never know that my entire life, I'd been drowning and now I was finally rising to the surface. I stared at her, then stared at Joe for so long that my eyes started to trace his soft freckled skin. I blurted out the best thing I could think of at the moment: "Oh, thank you for asking, but I really shouldn't ... maybe next time? I don't wanna hassle anyone, I—"

Mrs. Jennings interrupted. "Hassle? Dane ..." She frowned. "We'd love to have you. I won't hear anything else. Trust me, on chili nights, I *always* make too much, and Joseph over here doesn't have the biggest appetite." She flashed him a sympathetic smile. "So don't worry, all right?"

It beat the instant noodles my parents made me eat whenever the cold bitch didn't feel like cooking. Maybe this glimpse at love and stability would do me some good. Maybe gratitude for the moment was all I needed. Then again, the thought that none of this was *mine* and that, eventually, I'd have to go home flushed out all the momentary euphoria.

"All right, if it's no trouble ..." I said.

"None at all. I promise." Mrs. Jennings laughed. "Oh, but you should ask your parents, just in case. Go ahead and use the landline."

Talking to my parents was the last thing I felt like doing, but it was a weekend, and I wanted to spend as much time there as possible. I tried to placate them by fake-calling. I put in a random number and pressed my finger on the button to kill the call without them looking.

"Hey, Mommy ... yeah ... I was wondering if I could have dinner at Joe's. Yes ... I don't know ... Okay, love you" And then I paused for a few seconds, pretending to wait for her to say *I love you* back, something she'd never do. And then I hung up.

"Yes, they said yes."

"Fantastic!" Mrs. Jennings said.

Joe appeared to have become the Cheshire cat.

Joe asked me to stay the night. A sleepover. I ran home to get some clothes and raced back, winded and sweaty. I lied and said that I asked my parents' permission. They didn't care. One time I wandered outside the house all night. The sun had risen, and I walked in the front door when they were awake, actually wanting to get yelled at. They asked me if I'd taken the garbage out without any eye contact.

We stayed up eating ice cream and playing *Street Fighter*. He didn't spam. This in itself was cause for celebration. By the time we had to go to bed, I slid beneath the duvet on the extra futon they'd laid out for me.

"Thanks, Joe."

"For?"

"It feels good to not be alone tonight."

"No sweat, Dane."

He switched the lights off.

"Thanks too, Dane."

I thought he'd already gone to sleep. Hearing him whisper my name made my heart race. Was he, too, scared to sleep alone? Would he want me to climb into bed with him?

I closed my eyes but couldn't fall asleep. Through the window, car headlights blurred into narrow white swaths. It was a windy night, and the tree branches prattled against the roof.

What was this feeling?

I remembered what I found once as I was cleaning the house. My parents were out, and I was cleaning their room. Under my mom's bed, I found a tattered copy of Playgirl. I'd seen porno mags with naked women in my previous school, but this one was different. I was interested in these models. Looking at them made my chest feel a funny sort of way. All of them were brawny men. I skimmed the pages. Wanton-looking men lounged on ornate lounges and beside swimming pools. I couldn't help but feel something about their glistening skin, their stiffened cocks, and the way their inviting glances pierced through me from the page. I started to somewhat feel those same feelings again.

I wouldn't have minded getting into bed with Joe. I wouldn't have minded touching him and letting him touch me, holding him. I knew those thoughts were bad, but I couldn't stop the stirring in my chest when I was in such proximity to him. All I could do was whisper back:

"For what?"

"Before we moved here, my cat died. His name was Rex. He was my best friend. I had human friends, of course, but that cat lived and slept with me. I-I guess what I'm trying to say is, I'm glad you're here now."

"I'm glad too."

CHAPTER 9: NOW

Thud. Thud. Thud. The door slams open; its metal hinges screech with an ear-piercing frequency. The ravaged Joe barely looks and sounds like Joe is still there beside me, still straining to breathe. A petite silhouette stands next to the doctor. Is this someone else he kidnapped?

"Hey, boys. Meet Sadie. This little lady over here is pretty new, but she's got a mind that twists the same way as mine. Don'tcha, doll?" He bends down, and they suck face.

She steps into the overexposed studio lighting and flashes a lascivious smile. Her teeth are yellow-gray like she's smoked a pack a day since she was five. She's missing two in the front—it's a miracle any of them are still intact. Stringy black hair runs down her shoulders in ratty knots that frame her hideous face. Her forehead is creased like a child's papier-mâché project, and crow's feet ray out from her eyes. She has the physique of a crack addict: she'd unattractively thin, her bony shoulders and waist protruding from her stained off-white nurse's uniform (which looks like it was bought at some cheap sex shop). There is a leathery texture to her face, with sunspots from likely having spent too much time tanning. Her veiny forearms are lined with fresh needle tracks.

Sir runs a hand through her hair and then gives one of her sagging breasts a nice squeeze.

"Oh, Daddy, your hands are so naughty!" she chirps.

"Easy, kitty, don't wanna get you all worked up. I know how much you like to watch."

"I sure do." She looks at me and winks.

I want to vomit.

CHAPTER 10: FALL OF 2004

The fights between Mother and I escalated. The cold bitch was never interested in mitigating a tense situation between her and me; she just wanted to be right. I got home late? The bitch accused me of cutting class. I got a high grade on a test? The bitch would accuse me of having no life. Everything turned into how I was doing something wrong.

I'd try, hopelessly, to explain, but all that got me was a smack in the face. Whenever things got heated, whenever I attempted to calm things down, she fought back, and she fought back hard. I sat through her profanity-laced lectures like it was a nine-to-five.

She fought like she was unloading all her frustrations and stress on me because she married a man for the sole purpose of having the right to get fucked without the spinsters at church giving my nana shit. Our family looked good; I'll give it that. The lawn was ignored, and the tree was planted at an odd angle, sure, but overall, you'd never suspect that this was a loveless household. *Loveless*, however, was an understatement—we all fucking hated each other. Walk through the white picket fence and just past the front door and you'd find nothing but a disappointing facade curated by two people who defined marriage and love for me: an unending spiral of control, resentment, and fucked-up kids.

The worst thing about having divorced parents, to me, was becoming a cliche. Besides that, I couldn't care less if they each bit the tip of a shotgun, pulled the trigger, and took a permanent dirt nap. So what do you do when you're a powerless kid who can't move out? You do what I ended up making a semi-lucrative profession out of: grit your teeth, take it up the ass, and force all your disappointments to the back of your mind while telling yourself, *I'm fine; this is fine.*

It was one of those evenings when Dad had taken too long to come home. As punishment, Mom made me clean the entire house from top to bottom, told me what a shitty job I was doing, and yelled at me when I tried to tell her I was hungry and had to be up early for school. So much for being well-fed and well-rested. How was I supposed to get my grades up in that state? What fucking chance did I have?

The front door squeaked open. The rat bastard didn't announce his presence, but the loud thud and slamming door sure did. I smuggled a glass and one of Mom's protein bars upstairs so I didn't go to bed starving. Luckily, my bathroom had a tap with running water.

I ambled to the stairs to eavesdrop. They were speaking in hushed voices. They were cloaked mostly in darkness, save for the light from the streetlamp shining luminous, perpendicular lines on them through the slats.

"Why weren't you home when you said you would be?" Mom asked.

"You bring this up now, as I am trying to end my day in peace? Seriously? I told you I was going to be late today; what difference does it make?"

Dad flung the car keys into the ceramic bowl by the entrance.

"I don't know, it's only our fucking anniversary." She screamed that time.

"It isn't. Don't get brazen with me, Jen," he snarled, pacing himself between each word. "If this was so important to you, then maybe you would've at least taken the effort to look like you cared."

"What the hell are you implying?"

"If you weren't so numb in the head, you'd know that what I am saying isn't an implication; it's pretty fucking cut and dry." There he went, talking to her like she was a moron, not his wife. "I am saying you look like a fat slob!"

Her eyes widened as her cheeks flushed. "Well, unlike the pathetic whores you think about when you're fucking me—using my pussy as a hand, more like—I don't feel the need to cake my face with all that artificial crap!"

Oh boy, he hates it when she uses his condescending tone against him.

"You know what? That *artificial crap* is the only thing that keeps you from sweating like the dog you are!"

Dad was losing it. He punched the entrance table, shattering one of its legs, and the ceramic bowl with the keys and other trinkets smashed on the floor"

"Fuck! Fucking useless piece of shit!"

"You know what else is a useless piece of shit, huh?"

"Don't start, bitch. You couldn't even get the fucking abortion right. Now look what we're stuck with!"

"Oh, now you've done it, you asshole! Why don't you flip the whole fucking house over! Come on, show the whole world how pissed you are. Show them!"

He pointed his finger at her face and gave her an angry look.

"Oh, what, you think you scare me? Give me a fucking break. I want you to hit me so I can finally have an excuse to leave your sorry ass!"

Dad let out a derisive laugh and smacked his lips. "I'm done talking. Don't stay up for me."

He slammed the door to his study so hard that the entire house shook.

Abortion ...

I froze as Mom ascended the stairs. She noticed me as the two of us exchanged an uneasy glance.

"What the fuck are you still doing up?"

I ran up to her and hugged her by the waist. She stood there, stiff a board, not hugging me back. Instead, she grabbed a fistful of my hair and yanked it backward, forcing me to look up at her.

"I said, what the fuck are you still doing awake?" she hissed.

"Mommy, I didn't want you to be sad, I—"

Before I even finished that sentence, she smacked me so hard across the face, the blow sent me to the floor, and my knee caught the corner of the banister. The edge of the varnished wood cut into me, leaving a growing patch of what looked like red wine on the carpet. The stench of bourbon reeked on her; she was so drunk she didn't seem to notice the blood. Instead, she grabbed me by the arm—her nails dug deep creases into my skin—and threw me into my room.

I was too stunned to do anything. She'd yelled and sworn at me, but up until then, she'd never resorted to physical assault. I sucked in a deep breath, then took inventory of myself. The cut was still bleeding. I snuck into the bathroom and rinsed the gash under warm water and lathered it up with soap. I then pressed a clean old shirt onto it to stop the bleeding.

I had nasty dreams that night. My parents had cut me open and unspooled my intestines, stacking them into slimy clumps on my bed. Thick blood bubbled out of me like boiling rice gruel. They started with the intestines and then worked their way up to my lungs through my shattered breastbone. They tossed every organ to the side until I was left as hollow as I felt. They cackled the entire time.

I wished they had never gotten married. They could've easily spared each other all these years of frustration and unhappiness.

All they had managed to do was make my existence feel like nothing but a burden. All they talked about was money. If I was ever given a time machine, I'd go back to the day the old bitch chose to spread her legs and get cream-pied in that rotting clam between them. I'd grab her by her hair and tell her to do the world a favor and abort the baby. Hell, I'd do the procedure myself. I'd take a baseball bat to her head and bash her skull in so hard it would crack open like a cantaloupe. I'd slice her open and rip the disgusting sack of crying flesh out of her womb. I'd throw it to the floor and stomp on it as it writhed on the cold, hard tiles. I'd then throw it in the garbage, where it would undoubtedly live a more fulfilling existence than the one this cunt provided for it. Then I'd take my bat and use it to bludgeon that cunt's face in.

I remember jolting awake in cold sweats, crying so hard my throat went sore the following day. I could barely focus on school because of the overwhelming exhaustion. I must've only gotten three hours of sleep. I slept in the back of the classroom and thanked the universe that there was no PE that day.

I never took Joe home to meet the bitch that raised me. He and I always hung out at his place or down by the lake. Mrs. Jennings would make jokes, asking Mr. Jennings, "Where are my kids today?"—referring to both of us, of course. Joe wasn't an only child. He had an older brother and sister. He'd come along as a *surprise*, he told me. His older siblings already had lives of their own.

We went out into the woods that next afternoon and played hide and seek like a couple of idiots. The game had no rules, we could hear each other, and the person hiding would always give himself away by being unable to rein in his laughter.

"Found you!"

"No, I found you."

"You're so fucking bastard, Dane."

His misuse of the word *bastard*—and the seriousness with which he deployed it—made me laugh so hard I nearly pissed myself. I laughed so hard I couldn't even tell him what his error was; every time I tried to explain it, I ended up damn near busting a gut.

"Dane, seriously. Come on."

"That's not how you use that word, dipshit."

He made an angry face, which was so cute I began laughing again. His lips trembled, and I worried I was about to make him cry. Then he started laughing.

"Stop, I'm gonna fucking piss," he said.

He then focused his gaze on my leg. Thanks a lot, Mother dearest.

"Hey, what's that?"

His eyes were locked dead on the scab.

"It's nothing. Forget it, let's …"

He stopped my train though by kneeling down and lightly grazing the continent of scab tissue with his soft, silky fingers. I'd felt him brush up on me a couple of times, but I'd never had anyone I liked *touch* me like this. He continued to explore my leg, and a tingling sensation rose from my thigh to my groin.

My response was immediate and instinctual: I bent down and kissed him. It was just an innocent peck on the lips, but the electric current that jolted me back into the moment forced me to reel backward. His face was pale, and his mouth agape.

"I'm sorry," I said as my cheeks burned up seeing his blanched complexion.

"It's o-o-kay ... I ..."

I cast my gaze down and rubbed my shoulder, roughly massaging the building tension. It didn't work. The silence that followed was deafening. It was a bloated pause partially interrupted only by the sudden din of crawdads chirping to greet the auburn sky. My heart bucked against my ribcage like an alarmed steed. The back of my neck heated up as my entire chest constricted.

"Can I kiss you again?" I whispered, praying he wouldn't hear me through the song of dried leaves.

Against the noise, his answer came as a surprise.

"S-sure," he said.

I leaned in and kissed him again. He kissed me back. I kissed him and I kissed him and I kissed him. His lips parted and let me in. My tongue brushed against his. It felt so wrong, but I couldn't help but push in further. It stopped as both of us pulled back at the same time. I stood hypnotized, watching his lower lip tremble as he processed what had just happened. When he pulled away, a wet silver strand momentarily linked us like a fragile nerve between both our lips. I felt my love pulse through the liquid string, filling him with my need.

Daylight had faded into dusk. As our eyes adjusted to the absence of light, the details of the trees slowly materialized. Leaves took shape like memories—things I wish I'd said to him then. I knew he could feel my soul—my weakness without him by my side revealed itself. It was a kiss that both drained me and simultaneously filled me with the warmth of a home I never knew.

The clouds above us shifted like smoke from a factory, sealing the twilight sky in a gray blanket of gloom. The headlights of trucks cast glowing beams of light through the brambles and wooden cracks around us like migrating fireflies. They drove down the road with the thunderous noise of wildebeests being hunted. The sun slept in a cradle of night as everything began to turn deep blue.

Joe didn't look at me when he whispered, "We should head back."

We didn't speak on the way back to his house. When we got to his room, we played video games, ate pizza, and sat through a few commercials in silence. Yoko Kanno's incredible *Cowboy Bebop* score started playing on Cartoon Network. It was a Saturday, and we were allowed to stay up to watch the newest episode. Mrs. Jennings was cool about us watching PG-13-rated shows; she just turned a blind eye to it and said, "You boys have fun now," before bidding us goodnight. It was the fifth episode, the best one we had seen so far: "Ballad of Fallen Angels."

In the months that followed, I found myself thinking of Joe more and more. I found my thoughts drifting to him whenever I was alone. I shuddered at the thought, paranoid that he could secretly read my mind.

CHAPTER 11: NOW

Sir lays a gentle fingertip on my forehead and sweeps my wet bangs to the side. Sadie then bends down and kisses me. My stomach is knotted with anxiety, and the dried blood on me has turned clammy and itchy.

"Sugar, you're gonna be a good li'l boy now, ain'tcha."

"Her pussy gets real nice and wet whenever boys like yourself squeal like little piggies."

"Yes, he will; look at him!"

"All right, Fido. Allow me to remind you of the rules. If you don't partake in what I have planned for you, I'll cut something off him." He points his head at Joe. "Got that?"

A wave of fear floods over me, threatening to drag me with its undertow. He's secured me to a metal table; all my limbs are cuffed at the joint to each leg. There's no way for me to escape. The only other time I was this afraid was when Joe had gone missing. He left me once as a child and then another time as an adult, and now I fear that I am never going to see him again.

A sour tang of bile barrels up my throat as their hands fondle me, prod and poke at me as if I were a slab of meat being inspected at an abattoir. Sir jerks my head to the side and runs his hand down my chest, then up to my neck. A dollop of drool spills out of my mouth, and he swipes it away with one flick, sending it to the floor. Sadie reaches for something on the shelf.

"Sugar, you remind me so much of this bitch right here."

She holds something to my face, but my vision is still so blurred and bespeckled with black dots that I have to squint to see what it is: eyes and a slack-jawed mouth with a tongue so black and swollen it looks like a ball gag. One eye is looking right at me, while the other one is sewn shut. Dry blood is caked all over its face. The awful smell of decay roils into my senses as I fully register what she is holding up.

Piper.

She brings the corpse's decomposing head to her mouth and inserts her tongue into its maw, then begins sucking on its swollen tongue. She slurps in its juices; she bites into its tongue as a beige wad of spunk oozes out of it.

"Sadie here started playing with the heads she liked when she saw me going at it with a head."

She speaks as he walks onto the other side of the room and begins sharpening some blades. "Yes, Daddy, that's right! I was feeling lonely, and so I went to look for Daddy, and he was balls-deep in some blondie's head"—she stifles a laugh—"and get this,"—she nudges me like she's about to say the funniest joke ever known to man—"the head he was fucking wasn't attached to a body." And then she lets out a loud guffaw. She nearly drops the head in the process.

Well, I'm fucked.

These aren't people. They're on another level. They're unwell. How does anyone reach this level of humanity—or lack thereof?

Sadie places the head back into the metal bucket and moves to the foot of the metal table, beside him.

"You're such a good storyteller; I'm so proud of you." He grabs her by the back of her head, and the two begin to suck face right on top of my naked body. They've reached an abyss in their heads; these people can sleep at night and go back home to their families and face them after having done all of *this*. Through my fear and despair, I am quite awestruck by these two.

I'm sorry, Joe. I tried ...

I thought I knew pain, but what these fucking monsters are going to do to me isn't anything I've gone through before; it's something beyond my comprehension. They're not going to make small cuts deep enough to draw blood; they're going to fucking rip me open and enjoy it.

My thoughts go to my parents. The two people who, if I'd had a normal life, would come looking for me and send hordes of policemen and their bloodhounds on my trail. Perhaps seeing me like this wouldn't affect them at all—perhaps they don't even remember my face. They didn't care if I died a slow and dirty painful death then; they will not care now. Perhaps they'd be grateful for my killers because Sadie and Sir would have done what they'd tried to do to me before I was born. They'd wipe the earth clean of the smear they heaped upon it.

Scorching tears spill from the corners of my eyes and then off my face onto the table. I make another halfhearted tug at my restraints, but it's no use; my limbs are pulled so far apart I can't even flex them properly.

"What do you say we do first, Daddy?"

"Why don't you do that thing where you close your eyes and grab the first thing you touch?"

"Whee!"

Sadie spins three times and, once dizzy, reaches for something. She blindly gropes for the usual suspects: a set of needles, some hooks, genital clamps, an electric drill, a meat cleaver, a claw hammer, a cat o' nine tails, some scalpels, an assortment of blades and knives. She squeals with excitement as he congratulates her with a kiss on the cheek.

"Look at that pink little pucker, Daddy."

"I see. I wonder what we can fit in it."

I yell against the piss-stained gag. I scream against the gag so loud I tire my vocal cords out—I think they're going to need a week to recover.

"All right, Fido. We're gonna ask you once. Nod for yes, shake your head for no. If you say no, we're going to do it to your friend in the tub. Nod if you understand."

I nod.

"All right, Fido. May I cut off a part of you and feed it to you?"

A massive clump knots in my gut. I imagine breaking free of these chains and rushing him. I imagine tearing his eyes out with my nails. I can't see his face, but his gaze from the eye holes of his mask is obscenely lecherous. I shudder at the pain this is going to cause me, but there's no other choice. I can't allow Joe to—

"Three."

"Two ..."

The chains clang and bang as I nod aggressively.

In Sadie's right hand, she holds a pair of rusty scissors with serrated edges, presumably used to cut through meat. My flesh is no match for it. Sir takes my nipple in between his two fingers and pinches it, rolling it between his index finger and thumb. He bends down and licks it. Sucks it. At this point, I've resigned myself to whatever is going to happen. There's no point fighting. My skin pebbles with goosebumps.

He sinks his teeth into my raw flesh and clamps down, grinding from side to side. A hoarse scream tears out of my parched throat. I buck my hips upward, frantically trying to shove him off, slamming my tailbone back onto the metal and thrusting upward again. His bite only tightens. He chews down, then releases it. It's nearly separated from my body. The scissors cinch around the shredded tissue of my nipple and clamp shut, slicing it off. The pain comes immediately, in hot flushes so intense my entire throat constricts. Red streams race into the gutter below me.

And they're just getting started.

The entire room blurs as tears and sweat opaque my vision. My screams ricochet off the walls and boomerang back into my ears.

Something clicks, and the penetrating stench of gasoline quickly overwhelms the room. Beside me is a portable camping stove, and the meal of choice is me. Bile lurches up my throat, and its rancidness builds up to my uvula.

"Face the camera and open wide. Blow a bit; it's a bit hot," he says.

Sadie's loud chewing is nauseating.

"Yummy!"

"Did that taste good?"

"A bit tough, babe ... but yummy!"

I continue to sob profusely into the gag. My teeth chatter as I tremble. My chest burns like a brick has been smashed right in the center. My breathing comes in sips, not gulps.

"Daddy, I think we need to double-gag it." She smirks. "What's next, Daddy Sir?"

"I think we should introduce Fido to the magic water."

"The magic water? Already? Yippee!!"

Liquid sloshes around, hitting a container from side to side. Sir's form casts a shadow over me as he holds up a large container of something with both his hands. Behind him, Sadie is clapping and jumping for joy.

"Sadie, my dear, could you point the camera a tad bit lower?"

"Sure thing, Daddy Doctor Sir."

"Sorry for the delay; I don't want them to miss this. This is gonna hurt like a fucking bitch," he says.

He puts the container down and slips a cement block under my back, propping my dick and asshole up to face the lighting equipment. A cap is unscrewed, giving way to a cloying odor.

"We ran out of lube, so we're going to have to improvise."

I recognize the smell instantly: gasoline.

I scream louder and louder into the gag. Thrashing now, slamming my back up and down as Sadie grabs my hips and drives the small of my back down to the brick. Sadie parts my ass cheeks as Sir takes some of the gasoline and runs his gloved finger up and down my hole. Sadie holds something in front of my face.

"You're gonna stop resisting, and you're gonna act like you like it, Fido. Or else I'm gonna take this here lighter and set your friend on fire. Got that?"

I shrink inward and lie there, frozen.

"Blink once if you got that, you stupid fucking queer."

This time, he doesn't tell me what the task is. It takes all my remaining energy, but I relent. I blink.

He grips my hip bones and lifts me, probing the rim of my ass with more gasoline before plunging two fingers inside me. Without a moment's notice, he rams the tip of a plastic tube deep into me, breaking through the ring of muscle of my sphincter. My entire pelvic floor erupts in flames. The scorching sensation is so intense, the feeling is one of glass shards tearing into me. He thrusts the tube so far in, it's like he's about to give me a colonoscopy exam. The invasion stuns me into rigidity, making every muscle in my body spasm. I grind my teeth and scream into my gag.

"Now, Sadie."

My blurry eyes zone back into focus as he screws a funnel onto the other end of the tube. Sadie gets on her knees and opens wide as his fingers plunge into the back of her throat, gagging her. Butterflies combust beneath my core when I realize what's about to happen. She gags and leans over the raised funnel, vomiting directly into it. There is a shocking torment at the base of my spine, burning my colon the way it would if I tried to push out an acid shit. I grind my teeth together to prevent myself from sobbing, but it's all for naught. A scream catches in my throat as the chunky, boiling liquid sloshes inside me.

Sadie climbs on top of me. Bitter liquid careens down to my face. I strain to open my eyes after the fetid torrent has subsided, only to get a glance at the splayed lips of her warty cunt. Thin, uneven patches of wiry hair line her lesion-infested labia. She shakes as the last drops of concentrated piss drip right into my eye. Gurgling piss pushes through the lining of my throat.

The plastic tube is yanked out. A gastric fart, followed by a festering slop of shit, ejaculates in sporadic spurts out of me. Humiliating gas follows soon after.

Clop.

The tube and funnel fall to the floor.

Sir's hands grip my aching hips and repositions them. He then wheels the table to the side, shifting the angle so the camera is looking at us from the side now.

"Daddy, I wanna see you fuck him! Go on, fuck that little piggy," Sadie chants gleefully.

She lies on her bum and shoves her fingers in and out of her infected cunt, pleasuring herself.

"If that's what my baby girl wants, that's what my baby girl gets."

"Whee!"

"Fido, are you going to let Daddy fuck you? Or shall I fuck your friend's ballsack with a hunting knife?"

At this point, I'm too weak to resist. So I just nod.

His fleshy tip prods the cleft of my entrance. He clears his throat and spits a thick glob into his hand. He strokes himself at the sight of my ruined body. He then slams his dick into my damaged entrails, bucking forward and back.

I hoped that his dick would be easier to take than the vomit enema, but the feel of anything—no matter how soft—rubbing friction against my wounded cavity throws me into a new sphere of pain. It's unlike anything I could've prepared myself for. The rapid friction scrapes my walls like a rake. He digs his nails into my hips as he slams into me, literally fucking me to death. The muscles in my neck tense up as the thrusts build to a hellish crescendo.

Sadie then begins to drag a rusted knife over my chest, my remaining nipple, my stomach, and my limp cock. She pokes me with the handle of the blade, as if in search of the most tender part of a sacrificial lamb. It feels like my internal organs are trying to move, to hide from her blade.

"Now," he barks.

The menacing blade bites into the skin of my thigh. The burning pain happens all at once as the cold blade slides beneath my tissue and over the weakened membrane of muscle. The blade slides up and down, severing the rubbery tissue. The concentration of inflamed nerves comes to a head when Sadie yanks the flesh off and holds it above her starving maw. Blood drips onto her tongue.

"How does that taste, my love?"

"Dee-fucking-licious."

The wet patch of flesh brushes over me as blood drizzles my cheek. If my flesh were a map, this brand-new crimson archipelago would be a cartographer's dream.

The crispy sound of something frying is met with an aroma of fried meat. His chuckles rise as his Luciferic erection thrusts unabated into my rectum. He grunts as something hot squirts into my lower intestines. Hot piss fills my large intestines to the point of distention. His urine burns my unprotected flesh walls like salt to a wound. He then pulls his cock out of me, triggering a sudden release of my bowels. My sphincter spasms, expunging a stream of musky liquid.

"Aww, Daddy, looks like our little toy shat himself."

He stands next to Sadie and strokes the remnants of his erection. His cock is covered in my blood, his pubic hair matted with my light-brown, watery shit. He fondles Sadie's breasts as she cooks.

He unfastens my gag and sets it aside. The second it's out of my mouth, acid gurgles past my lips, and I jerk my head sideways to retch, releasing a load of bile to the floor. I gag and cough as the rest of the vomit runs down the left corner of my mouth.

I try to scream, but the back of my throat is so dry all I can muster up is a silent, breathy rasp followed by another series of dry coughs.

Sadie cradles the side of my head and forces something past my lips. The rich, savory flavor has a sweet undertone. My gut cramps with sudden hunger pangs; it gives me the illusion that this is the best thing I've ever tasted. I chew and swallow so recklessly that I nearly gag again. If I could have it my way, I would've rather choked right then and there.

Sadie licks the vomit down the side of my chin, then sucks the open flesh wound where my nipple used to be. The pain is so intense my grasp of the world around me—my command of consciousness—flickers in and out.

They share the meat they've excised. Sadie holds it up to him with her teeth as he bites off a portion. Their lips lock in an unholy kiss.

I fade into a weightless vacuum. The hope of death soothes me; I am returning to a home I'd never known, to a place where I can rest forever. To the lake. To the last summer I was happy. My heavy eyelids slip shut.

Do what you want to with this corpse, with this body. It's not mine. I didn't choose life in the first place—life just happened to me. At last, I sink into the yawning abyss. My last thought is about Joe. It's a memory of when—

CHAPTER 12: FALL OF 2004

—he vanished a couple of weeks before I was about to start fourth grade. Joe told me he was going to be moving in the second week of September. We'd spent so much time together, and I'd even helped him pack some of his boxes. My parents and I visited this lake in Canada called Lake Placid for the week so they could "rekindle their relationship." I was, once again, secluded in my room watching television. I wondered what Joe thought of the most recent *Cowboy Bebop* episode.

The bitch and the rat bastard hardly spoke the entire time.

Summer fizzled out, giving way to the scent of fresh melons and ripened squash. Autumn cast its shadow, bringing forth bony tumbleweeds and fragments of gummy sap. Cicadas hummed their songs as dead leaves skidded through the town's streets like petulant forest sprites. The days became shorter, and the nights came with a bitter chill. On the drive home, Mom and Dad maintained their silence. I leaned my head on the shaky window, watching as migrating birds danced in the sky with the subtle elegance of synchronized swimmers. The band on the radio crooned sad folk songs through static signals.

When we got back, Joe was gone. His house was empty. I searched everywhere for a note that didn't exist. I dug through all my drawers, searched under my pillow, and scoured the roots of the trees in the woods. Nothing. I tried the landline, and some kid who wasn't him answered. Joe was gone, and there was no way to reach him. I tried my best to banish him from my head. The harder I tried to forget him, the more I fell into the reverie of our time together. The ache in my chest was a stab to the heart that kept prying deeper even when I thought it had already reached its limit. The things we want to forget, we remember, and the things we want to remember, we forget.

Fuck it all to hell.

The only question I had was: why? Why didn't he want to be friends with me anymore? I had the same landline, and he could've called. I thought he and I were friends. Was it my friendship that pushed him away?

What did I do to let him down? Did he know how much this hurt me?

My parents didn't want me. They paid for my stuff, yes, but they only did so to shut me up. Telling themselves that they were sustaining my life—through money— was them validating themselves. Every day that I hadn't starved to death was an opportunity for them to pat themselves on the back. I never once heard the words "I love you" come from either of them.

I'd poured all my love into Joe without his consent. I depended heavily on his approval, on his companionship, on him ... even if it was just platonic. His friendship, the mere fact that someone, anyone, would willingly spend time with me, meant the world to me. Now all I had was me.

And I've never fucking liked me.

Forcing myself to part with him was like cutting a part of myself off. I poured all my appreciation into others, and all they ever did was walk away with all I'd given them. Taking and taking, and leaving me. Joe was the first person I can ever say I truly loved. Perhaps not romantically but in a way that made me feel at home. I missed home so much.

Seeing the Jennings' house empty was like being thrown into ice water without any warning. I sank in slow motion. The wind chills stabbed into my pores and gnawed at my bones. I sobbed and begged to be spared. Nothing came to save me. It was ice all the way down; it's been ice all the way down for as long as I can remember. Perhaps I threw myself into the ice water? Perhaps if Joe was here, he would've held me back. He would've said:

"Don't worry, Dane. I've got you. And I'm not letting go."

CHAPTER 13: FALL OF 2004

I lay in bed, under covers so heavy you'd think it was mid-winter. The weather was gloomy; the rain pattered on the glass of the window pane. The light of the moon cast a long rectangle on the foot of my bed. Above me, a neon constellation of pasted stars and planets shimmered. My exhausted gaze was fixed on the rings of Saturn. I yawned as the constellation over my head blurred in and out of focus. I prayed that the ceiling would disappear, that gravity would cease, and that I would float up into the stars and be held in the eternal embrace of the endless night sky.

A jangling doorknob jolted me into alertness. A thin line of light materialized across the other end of the room. The door was slightly ajar. Whoever was standing behind it inched it open. My entire body locked up with anxiety as I recoiled into my mattress, hoping that it would swallow me up before—

"How is my special boy today?"

I smelled him before I saw him. The stench of bourbon invaded the room.

The alarm clock read 4:11 a.m. Panic raced through every inch of me. The rain intensified, pelting the window like a fistful of pebbles. My breath caught in my throat as my heart raced. I gripped the sheets so hard my knuckles whiten.

"Is my special boy doing well this morning? I came an hour earlier; this gives us a few hours before the bus gets here."

His shadow loomed over me as he stood by the foot of my bed. The left side of the bed sank as the weight of his knee landed on the mattress. The coarse hair on his arm swept my cheek as his rough palm found the bare flesh of my gut. The pads of his prodding fingers grazed their way up to my chest. I flung my arms forward to shake him off. "*Stop!*" I yelled into his sweaty palm.

"You shut the fuck up, you little shit," he growled, inches away from my face, his closed fist held up to me.

Trying to fight him off was like kicking a punching bag made of steel. Something wet trailed down my neck; its warmth came with the pungent stench of whiskey and smoke. My chest deflated as tears welled up in my eyes.

"You don't have a choice, you little shit. Daddy's house, Daddy's rules."

All the hope I had that my pleas would get to him was shattered.

"Actually, the reason I'm here is because your fat bitch mother thinks her golden cunt is too good for me. I've watched you grow up ... I wonder if your prick has grown as fast as you have."

He grunted and let out a cough.

"Fuck, Dane, your skin is so soft. I remember when your mom felt this good. I wish you didn't have a dick, though. But you've got a nice tight hole back here. And still no leg hair. Yeah, this is gonna fucking work ..."

I gritted my teeth and struck him in the face with my closed hand. I bit down on the hand clamping my mouth shut. I ground my teeth until I tasted blood. The slap landed hard on the side of my face; bells and sirens rang in my head. My neck was pinned down by his girthy forearm, choking me as I gasped for air. His disgusting tongue slid all over my neck and chin. He forced my mouth open with his fingers and licked me.

"Mmm. Good boy, looks like you didn't forget to brush your teeth."

I had half a mind to eat my shit and keep it there if he ever tried this again.

I cried out, gasping for air as I coughed and choked on my spit. He spat on his right hand and slid his hand beneath the waistband of my pants. Despite my physical protests, he stayed in place, resolute. The rings of Saturn blurred out of focus behind my scalding tears.

Thunder cracked as the patter of rain struck the roof so loud, you'd think it was hail falling. I yelled so loud my throat damn near could've bled. I twisted and wrenched, desperately trying to break free as his hand slid down my pants.

"Say you're my good boy."

He lifted his forearm slightly, and I let out a wail.

"Oh, so that's how this is going to be, eh? Fuck, your crying makes me hard."

His visits initially only happened once a week; they then occurred almost every other night. He watched me in bed and stood by the door, a spectral silhouette against the light of the hallway. He stood there, peering at me in the darkness the whole time. The silence of the room made his breathing more audible; his deep, sodden inhales were laced with carnality. Occasionally, I'd hear the distinct rubbing and grunting sounds he made as he pleasured himself.

I suspected he probably crushed a valium into Mom's drink to send her off to Dreamland. This gave him the luxury of being uninterrupted. She wouldn't know what hit her until the next morning. Even when she did, she'd just suspect she had a hangover from the night before.

The closer he walked to me, the more pungent the smell of bourbon on his breath was—it had been his drink of choice. The old bitch hadn't been in a bad mood in a while because he hadn't been in a bad mood. He dictated the entire mood of the house: that all depended on how well I performed.

Whenever I did fall asleep, my dreams were a montage of his face looking down at me, his features distorted in harrowing ecstasy.

I considered opening up to guidance counselors and teachers, but the shame and guilt stopped me every time I tried. When I walked home from school, I had thoughts of walking into a stranger's house and pretending to live there. In my daydream, nobody said anything. The friendly couple who owned the house was a little surprised at first, but they smiled anyway. They were nice people. They told me they'd always wanted a child but could never have one. They told me I was beautiful and that the spare room upstairs was mine if I wanted it. They set a place for me on the dinner table and asked me how my day was. They didn't cast shame and judgment on me. After dinner, I went upstairs and brushed my teeth as the new mom moisturized her face beside me and the new dad fixed his suit for work the next day. I then slipped under the covers of the softest bed I've ever lain in and slept a profoundly restorative sleep.

Daydreams can be dangerous ... especially when you wake up and life happens.

One night at dinner, the two were engaging in a jovial conversation. One that I drifted in and out of as I sipped my ramen noodles on the couch, as far away from them as I could be. I normally scheduled my meals at different times (read: whenever the kitchen was empty) to maintain the illusion of my daydream, but tonight it couldn't be helped.

"Hey, Dane, get over here."

I ambled over and took a seat at the small, circular table. The hot noodles took an eternity to cool down. I contemplated slurping them up anyway—scalded tongue be damned—but I knew that would get commented on. My entire body strained as Dad's hand ran up my lap. Mom was completely oblivious to it; her gaze was lost in his as he regaled her with his work day. I sat there, wanting to drop dead. I could hear myself screaming but only in my head. She ought to thank me for him being in a good mood.

"Dane, pass the peas."

And I did. My spineless self, too small to stand up to these giants. He asked me something, but everything sounded like it was being said underwater.

"What?" I said cuttingly.

"Why are you so hostile? Here I am trying to have a conversation with you, and you're being fucking rude."

"When did you become such a brat?" the bitch added.

I didn't say anything. I didn't look up. I knew they couldn't read minds, but if they could, they'd know I wanted to kill them both. I wished the plastic cup of noodles in front of me was laced with arsenic. It would at least give me the quickest, easiest escape.

"You are an ungrateful shit, you know that?" Dad said.

"He's like an animal."

"He will never amount to anything with that attitude."

I stayed silent. What the fuck else could I do? I fixed my gaze on my lap, forcing myself not to glare back at them. Their gazes bore down on me, actively hating me. To them, I was an animal who'd never amount to anything. That's a parent's love for you. I stood up and started toward the stairs.

"Dane."

"Yes?"

"You haven't asked to be excused."

I exhaled and clenched my teeth. "May I please be excused?"

Before I could suck in my next breath, Dad sucker punched my gut so hard I fell to the floor. The blow knocked all the air out of me; a warm patch formed on my crotch and ran down my leg. I pissed myself in the living room. In front of me was the door; past the door was ... Wait. He was gone. The only place I could run to—my refuge from all *this*—was no longer there.

"Feeling any friendlier yet, boy?" the rat bastard said.

He'd never hit me like that before. Not like that. He had whipped me before, sure, but he'd never punched me. This was new, even for Dad. Mom didn't scream. She didn't get up to see if I was all right. She didn't yell at him and swing her fists, cursing him out for having the gall to punch a fucking ten-year-old boy. His son. Their son. She didn't ask him why he hit me. Instead, when I looked up, I caught a sly smirk on her face.

"Disgusting. Be sure to clean your mess up," is all she said.

I never got used to Dad's visits. I refused to cry for him; the rat bastard was not getting one single tear. I just lay there and let him at me, no longer under the illusion that he'd snap out of his drunken stupor and realize what he was doing to his child. Eventually, I stopped smelling booze on him; he raped me while he was stone-cold sober. All I wanted was mercy, some semblance of human warmth. I didn't get so much as a squirt of piss out of a dead cow's pussy.

"I'm gonna make some money out of you."

He grabbed my hair and jerked my head around because my helplessness and screams helped get him off. The entire room blurred behind the thin film of tears. He started getting off even when he pressed down on my stomach hard and masturbated as I vomited in my toilet. The thought of my throat being invaded—even if it wasn't by his cock—helped get him off. He made sure to tape everything.

He'd throw me on the wall so hard the thud would reverberate throughout the entire upstairs.

"Quiet up there!" Mom would yell.

"Shut up!" Dad would bark back.

Eventually, he stopped drugging her. She'd no doubt heard enough to infer what was happening behind my bedroom door. The two had some sort of agreement, it seemed. He could do whatever the hell he wanted as long as he stayed out of her way and treated her well.

That's not to say that he stopped using drugs altogether—he started using them on me.

Across the room, Dad set up a tripod and mounted his camcorder on it. He wanted to capture everything he was doing to me. When the flash turned on, he slipped on his hockey mask and made me kneel in front of him.

"Here, sniff this. Sniff all of this up."

He grabbed me by the hair and held a hand of white powder to my nose. After several tries, I managed to force the white substance through my nasal passages. It was a fine powder that smelled like paint thinner. My face went completely numb, then an unwanted sense of excitement and adrenaline kicked in. Sparklers cracked and burst in my head. I began to crave the euphoric drip of liquid down the back of my throat. Dad did this to keep me up all night so I wouldn't feel the exhaustion foisted upon me after a long, arduous day at school.

"Open wide," he'd say before pissing on my face. I coughed most of it up, but he wasn't satisfied unless I drank what was in my mouth. The jaundiced fluid tasted as bitter as bile laced with sea salt. He then slapped the tip of his cock on my tongue to get the excess piss droplets out.

"Don't you just love being my little underage slut?"

I nodded because what else could I do? What fucking chance did I have against this monster?

"You will only know a life of filth, my little fuck-slut. Mommy and I don't love you. We never did. Got that? Now bend over."

He yanked my boxers down and probed the rim of my asshole with his thumb. He nudged into it a bit, but it didn't give. He spat on his hand and returned to me, finally pushing past the tense ring of muscle. A fire ignited in my pelvis. I bit into my bottom lip to stop the screams. Briny tears pierced my eyes. He loved the screams and the sobs.

"Fuck, that's a nice hole."

He pulled out and pushed his fingers into me, twiddling his index finger in such a way that made a warm throb pulse deep in my stomach. He pulled out his fingers, spat on his hand, and slammed his dick into my hole again.

"That's what this fucking hole was made for, boy." He grunted as he slammed into me. No matter how many times he did it, it never failed to hurt. It felt like I was being penetrated by a cock made of dry, jagged stone. Every time he pulled back, it felt like he was shearing a patch of tender rectal tissue. My spine bent backward, threatening to snap.

Then his arm came down, curving at full speed and force through the air. His fist bashed against my head. His arm rose again, striking me in the face. Blood squirted all over the bed sheets. Despite the tears and blood, his cock stayed inflated inside me. He pushed my face into the mattress, cutting out my air supply before yanking my head up. I gasped for air. He pummeled my back, vacuuming the fresh air from my lungs. He punched me a fifth and sixth time. The noise rebounded through my head like a wet smack. His body stilled, and he grunted; hot, thick spurts bulleted deep into my guts. He pumped so deep into me it felt like his cum was going to trickle into the pit of my stomach. My mouth was open. I was trying to scream, yet all I managed to produce was hot air. My body sizzled and spasmed throughout the violation.

He took the camcorder and started taping me at a closer angle. People would watch this: a scene of an innocent's destruction rendered through a misty filter. He'd never fucked a guy in the ass before me, so we'd had a few accidents. He ripped into me so hard I shat all over the floor. I passed out from the pain. When I woke up, he had collected all the shit and vomit into a bucket and held my head to it. It was filled with brown and creamy fecal matter congealed with undigested food.

"Now, eat it."

I tried to tell Mom about the abuse, but she did nothing. I had nothing to do and no one to turn to. To numb the pain, I took to cutting myself. I hid one of Mom's kitchen knives in my bathroom and made small incisions on my thighs and arms.

One of my earliest memories was when I was still in kindergarten. I'd decided to take a potato peeler to my finger just to see what could happen. I was mesmerized yet completely unperturbed by all the blood. There had always been something so perverse and alluring about thinking of my body as mere meat.

I remember falling asleep on my right arm one time in class and waking up to discover it had gone completely numb. It was like someone else's arm lay in front of me. The first time I cut myself, I stabbed my thumb down to the bone. Before dressing the wound, I pried it open with a tweezer and rifled through the layers of muscle visible to me.

Bodily damage had since become something intimate, almost sexual. I started doing it regularly to distract myself from the feral beasts in my head. To have complete autonomy over my pain confronted me with the boundary between "me" and "my body," the notion that my body was a piece of meat to be sliced open.

Dad saw the cuts I made and decided he wanted to make a few of his own. He tied my wrists to the bed frame and tore my shirt off. I cried, screamed, and begged ... yet all that did was make his cock harder. He held the camcorder above me with his left hand and held a safety pin in right. He didn't even bother disinfecting it before digging the metal into me. It burned the way I would imagine it would if surgery was performed without any anesthetic. The sheets were a bloody mess by the time he was done. It was only when I was in the shower that I saw that he had written something across my stomach: *I AM A DIRTY SLUT.*

And was he wrong?

Dad stopped filming me after a couple of months of having his fill. He'd probably saved up enough from the movies of us he made. It started again when I was about 14, but by that time, I'd grown taller and would exercise after school. I stole a baseball bat from the PE closet and hid it under my bed. At that point, I'd played enough baseball and had enough upper body strength to bat a fifty.

I waited until he'd finished on me before taking the bat out and swinging it so hard at his junk he fell to his knees.

"You ... fuck you ... I'm going to call the cops on you; they'll lock you up for life."

He got up and attempted to tackle me, but I smashed my knee on his nose. His cartilage made a meaty, crackling sound as a torrent of blood gushed out. His fists pounded the floor as he groaned in agony. He then spewed out a torrent of curses and snarled at me with eyes so paralyzing I nearly froze. Veins protruding from his temples reminded me of pulsating roots.

"You're dead. You're fucking dead!"

I was done taking his shit. What did he think was going to happen? He was on the floor, squeezing his smashed nuts and glowering at me. His look was priceless (I've still never seen such a pathetic expression on someone's face). I snapped forward, a wee inch away from his face.

"When you call the cops, would you mind telling them whose cum is all over my underwear inside that plastic bag?"

He glowered at me, shaking as the bubble of his inflated self-worth popped. I didn't break my piercing glare. I looked him dead in the eyes like I was staring down the barrel of a gun. I knew that this was my life now. It was either fight or die.

His punch connected so fast blood instantly leaked out of my nose like a busted pipe. I was used to pain. What I wasn't used to was the deadly take-no-prisoners fury that burned through me as I swung the bat directly at his face. The sound of cracking branches gave way to yowling. At that point, I didn't care if he died. Heck, I'd kill Mom too. I'd find a way to get away with it. Dead crackers told no tales.

Dad fumbled backward and raised his arm, motioning for me to stop, begging for mercy. Yeah, fuck mercy. I climbed on top of him and clobbered the rat bastard piece of shit with everything I had. He rolled over, and I rained blow after blow down his back like I was beating nothing more than a sack of sand. This feeling of power certainly wasn't something I was used to, yet it was nonetheless refreshing.

Dad left for the hospital that night, never to return.

Mom blamed me.

In the middle of high school, I ran away.

CHAPTER 14: SUMMER OF 2011

A thin bed of dry leaves flanked the corners of the swing. The playground was empty at that time in the morning. I took off my cap and ruffled my hair. The idea of trading money for sex both excited and terrified me. But I was left with no other choice.

About five truckers drove by before one stopped. I swung back and forth, pretending not to notice, but I did. I didn't care what they did to me. The second it started, my mind would just drift to all those summers ago. To the sun-dappled lake. I flitted a furtive glance at the lowered window, searching for any scrap of human warmth in their eyes. (I never found any. Their emotions always vacillated from lust to guilt.)

I squinted at the driver, taking in weary eyes and a red mustache. A finger poked from the crack of the passenger seat window, beckoning me to approach him.

Hook, line, and sinker.

"You got cash?"

"Yeah, how much will a fifty get me?" he asked. He must've had a thing for jailbait if he was already offering such a sum right off the bat.

"It'll get ya whatever you want."

"Hop on in, then."

He said his name was Jarred. He'd been divorced a couple of times and was on wife number three. He had two kids, both boys with their own lives. "You look a bit like my second, Johnny," he said in a gravelly monotone. "I've always wanted to try some things on him, you see. But I'm a good man. I'd never put my hands on my son."

I take a good whiff of his cab; it smells just like my dad's study. Hopefully, this guy's not on the juice now. All I need is a fucking truck accident. He must've read my mind because he offered me his flask. I took it, unscrewed the lid, and sipped. It tasted like fire water. I coughed a couple of times before taking another few sips. His hand fidgeted on his mustache, then scratched at his chin. I slid closer to him, and he placed his hand on my bare thigh, massaging it.

The corners of his windshield were a graveyard to dead midges, mayflies, and moths. Their bodies left a gray paste across the glass along with wing and antennae residue. The highway ahead of us stretched on forever.

The air conditioning unit was broken, so he rolled the window down. In came a gust of summer air.

We stopped at a gas station on the outskirts of Nebraska, filled up the truck with gas, and bought a cherry coke to share between the two of us. Across from the gas station was a crummy motel with a neon blue *vacancy* sign.

"Let's get a room for the afternoon, son."

The bed in the motel was stiff, and the room had the rank stench of mildew. The sickly green bedspread showed a few patches of brown stains. Across from us was a boxy television set that looked as if it had been collecting dust for years.

I unbuttoned my shorts and slid them down my waist.

"No, no. Don't rush, son. Go slower." He knelt in between my legs and started to massage my thighs. He placed his hand on my chest and willed me to lie on the bed. I didn't touch him; he took full control. He slid my shorts down and slipped three fingers under my briefs. He then pinched at my nipples as he rubbed my crotch through the white cotton. He lowered himself, stopping when his head was over my lap. His tongue found my soft cock. He teased it alive, licking it like it was a cold treat.

I naturally thought of Dad. How my encounters with him compared to this. Those nights may have happened many moons ago, but they were burned fresh in my head. By now, I'd lost count of how many men I'd been with. I didn't mind, as long as I didn't have to go back home. While Dad's hands brutalized me, this man's hands sensually caressed me. And then he looked up at me.

"Hey, kid. Is something wrong?"

"No."

"You're barely hard."

He took me in his mouth again, hastening his movement. He sucked and slurped as I forced myself to recall the men in my mom's Playgirl magazine. Where they were hard, he was soft; where they were smooth, he was hairy. His mouth was so much warmer than Dad's. His teeth lightly grazed against my length, but that was to be expected. He was probably new at this; who was I to judge? He ran his hands down the back of my calves as he pressed his nose to my pubic bone. His lips clamped around my balls, taking both of them into his mouth at the same time.

And then I felt it.

"Hey, I'm almost ..."

He didn't pull his head back. I tried lightly patting his head, but he didn't move. I flinched as my climax rushed down my spine. I gripped the bedsheets as he sucked me harder, chasing my orgasm. It couldn't be helped. I spilled down his throat as he enthusiastically slurped up and swallowed every last drop.

He got up, opened his wallet, and chucked a fifty at me. This cold and transactional exchange was what I was used to. Normally, they wanted to blow me, but I didn't mind sucking cock. I'd rather have a cock in my mouth than a cock in my ass. Unless, of course, they stuck it in my ass then forced me to put it in my mouth.

It went on like this for years. I don't remember much of it. All these images just blurred into one another.

I wrote a couple of ads in bathroom stalls: "Free all day. Ready to please. Up for anything. Young, willing, affordable, and discreet. Meet me at the gas station parking lot."

The sun was out in full force that day, so I waited under a plum tree. Overgrown weeds tickled my calves as mosquitoes helped themselves to my naked legs. The sweet odor of ripening plums permeated the summer air. When day turned to night, I looked up and soaked in the clear night sky; stars glittered in the blackness, uninhibited by light pollution.

The cool air smelled like mosquito repellent and hamburgers from the diner across the street. Johns wouldn't come by much on weekends since there wasn't much of an excuse to be out of the house and not be spending time with their families. I had nowhere to sleep and rarely had anything in my belly.

My crotch had been bothering me for some time, so I inspected myself in the bathroom. Unsurprisingly, my dick was bruised from all the rough-handling I permitted. My shaft was purple, and my inner thighs were scarred with red bite marks and cigarette burns. Upon closer inspection, I noticed tiny peppercorns beneath the curls of my pubic hair. I scrubbed at them, pinching them away and wincing as their whisker-like legs grasped onto my pubis for dear life.

This didn't stop the Johns, though. Lucky me.

There were some bubbles of joy being on the road alone, though. Not all the Johns were old fucking creeps. Not all of them wanted sex either. A handful of them just wanted to feel less lonely. They'd tell me stories about how their kids hated them for being failures—for being unable to provide any time for them because they were stuck working to put food on the table. They just wanted someone to keep them company, someone to hold and listen to their apologies as they wept into the night.

I wished they'd adopt me. Their kids didn't know how good they had it.

This one guy asked me if I'd go to the movies with him. All his children had grown up, and he was home alone. I found it ironic how he was stuck longing for the past while I was here doing everything in my power to escape it. We stopped by a Drive-In Theater that had opened for the summer, illuminated with bright lights at the marquee. I leaned on his shoulder as a restored Victor Fleming film played from the projection booth.

He took me to a motel after the film and allowed me to keep my clothes on. He merely requested that I watch as he undressed. He was overdressed for the summer, and his button-up shirt was a few sizes too big. Rail thin wouldn't be an accurate description for him—the man was utterly emaciated. His joints protruded from his milky skin; his ribs reminded me of a rack used to wash clothes. His chest was adorned with dark lesions and crusty boils.

"I'm a sick man," was all he said.

I didn't know what he meant then.

He paid enough for penetration, but he assured me we'd play it safe. I sipped the sweat from his navel like it was fetid water. I licked his back, washing over the ridges of disease and swollen growths. I dived into his pubic mound and took his bent cock in my mouth, worshiping it like it was a source of water in the midst of an arid desert.

He then got on his forearms and arched his back, pointing his ass toward me.

"Make your hand look like a duck's beak and slide it inside me with the baby oil. Make Daddy happy."

I reached toward his underside, running my greasy fingers along his bony ass. I entered him, feeling a meaty organ and mass of tender gut coiling around my fingers. I pried my fist into his warm canal, probing deeper inside. His innards were warm and damp like the flesh of a slug; they coiled around my wrist and sucked at my hand. I moved further inside his body as he groaned in pleasure, moving his entrance closer to my elbow. It felt like I had plunged my entire arm into a tight sleeve of muscle tissue.

He paid for the room and left me to sleep in it by myself.

My last client was a man named Novak. He recognized me from some videos he saw circulating online. He showed me one of them: it was of me and Dad. He said there was a huge market for those sorts of videos on the dark web and that they fell under the category of "hurtcore." He explained that sick fucks traded these types of videos online—films of children being sexually abused and brutalized. All things considered, at least Dad left me with all my limbs intact. Novak said he was recruiting kids my age and offered to house me if I agreed to work for him. I was happy to oblige.

Thanks for finding me a job, Dad. Wherever you are, I hope you give yourself a good pat on the back for being good for something.

CHAPTER 15: SUMMER OF 2019

My apartment sat on the fifth floor of a grungy building. The streets were never silent. Dogs barked, kids screamed, and drug dealers lurked around every corner. As I sat on the rooftop admiring the sunset, the air smelled of smoke and overcooked hotdogs. I blew a cloud of smoke out at the spires of distant buildings glowing against the dull azure sky. The final rays of sun cast golden edges to the silhouettes of the skyscrapers at my feet. When I returned to my apartment, I lay in bed under sweat-dampened sheets infested with crumbs and half-eaten pizza. The television served as my only source of light, tunneling through the oppressive shadows.

Novak was pissed. Rent was due this month, and I'd been slacking. Although he made me escort on the side, the quickest way to make money was the shit I did online. Whether I was getting fucked or fucking myself didn't make a difference as long as I got paid. Webcam modeling cast a wider net because you could perform a show to several paying customers as opposed to just one; you could even start an all-out bidding war and have one person buy you for all you were worth. Tricking people into thinking you're worth something was always so much fun.

Novak found me when I was hooking from city to city, motel to motel. He didn't mind that I'd been sucking dirty cocks all day and getting gut-pounded by unwashed truckers like a seasoned lot lizard after just having hit puberty. He was one of Dad's many clients who jerked off to videos of my father ass-raping me. I was Novak's favorite. He told me he had no problem shooting out a massive wad of nut snot whenever I was on screen.

One of the websites he made me go on was called Chaturbate. There were two domains on the site: Public Chat and Private Chat. You could be nude on public chat and pretty much do whatever. I didn't have enough to pay for a gym membership; a face as cherubic as mine needed an adolescent body to match it anyway. Public chat was my preference; I used it to sift through those who were truly interested.

The tips fluctuated on the day of the week. I got most tips on Mondays because that's when people were most in need of having their self-esteem raised.

People sometimes sent me things they wanted me to wear. More than a few men lied to their families about donating their son's small clothes to charity only to send them to me. They called me "son" and watched me take the clothes off and call them Daddy.

I hated talking, but I did love coming up with stories for my clients—my imagination was a roller coaster. I told them what they wanted to hear and showed them what they wanted to see. Novak gave me free rein to come up with scenarios to get his clients off. That was always the most fun part.

[Oliver636 has requested a private chat] 50,000 tokens.

FIDO [Accept]

I made the first move since he was nice enough to give me a token tip that was equivalent to $500.

CHAT ROOM:

FIDO: Hi

OLIVER636: How are you, what's up.

FIDO: Nothing much, you?

OLIVER636: Not much, boring this morning.

FIDO: Wanna have some fun, Daddy?

OLIVER636: we could
OLIVER636: how old are you, son
FIDO: 16, if that's okay
OLIVER636: nice nice
FIDO: What you in the mood for
OLIVER636: jerk?
FIDO: ok daddy
OLIVER636: cool!
OLIVER636: sory, im new here how does this work?
FIDO: you tell me what to do, and I do it
OLIVER636: take off your shirt
OLIVER636: mmmm
OLIVER636: sexy
FIDO: u like?
OLIVER636: looking good son ;)
FIDO: I hope you're touching yourself
OLIVER636: get that dick nice and hard boy
OLIVER636: common son show me something ;)

And show him something I did. A stack of textbooks and pencils lingered in the background. I spread my legs, aiming my crotch at the camera. I rubbed my dick above my tight shorts, reveling in the thrill of an older man's eyes on me. This pervert likely imagined that I was his underage son. He probably got the first boner his middle-aged ass had gotten in years watching his little boy make O-faces at him. *Yes, you pervert, I am your kid ... Watch me as I do something dirty. Something that I only do when no one is watching. It's all for you, Daddy.*

I clumsily slipped off my school blazer and revealed that I wasn't wearing an undershirt. Beneath the polyester was my hairless chest. He didn't even mind the mural of lesions and scar tissue. I tweaked my nipples, making them pebble. I unhooked my belt and licked my fingers, rubbing my dick with one hand.

Then my phone vibrated.

NOVAK: Kill this show, I've got a client that wants you. Red Den. Now.

[NOTIFICATION] The Red Den: "You have a request for a private room session. 10k. Den code: J973hKHho8w.

Finally, something challenging. I refunded Oliver and apologized. I fired up my TOR browser and entered the dark web. I then headed on over to The Red Den to input the room code. I normally played to an anonymous audience, but this time, I saw a basement. A man in a white, featureless mask sat completely naked. He was more well-built than the kind of guy you'd expect to see on here. The lights in the basement were all red like the light bulbs had been drenched in blood.

He spoke, startling me. I didn't know viewers on this site had the option to talk.

"Hi," he said with the gravelly voice of a lifelong smoker.

"Hey,"

"Age?"

"Guess."

"You don't look a day over seventeen. Heck, if you told me you were sixteen, I'd believe you."

"I won't tell if you won't, Daddy."

"Daddy, huh?"

"What shall I call you, then?"

"They call me the Puppetmaster. You, however, may call me Sir."

"All right, *Sir*."

"Good boy."

"What would you like, Sir?"

"I'd like to make you bleed, and I want you to like it."

The amount of hair on his body told me that he was at least in his mid-thirties. Scars littered his chest. Ones that I recognized because they looked self-inflicted.

Almost like mine.

"Come closer. Show me your arms."

I crawled up to the webcam and raised my wrists to it. Three large scars lined my forearm; five parallel lines bisected them on the flesh patch that rarely sees sunlight. You could hardly tell where one cut started and another one ended. I'd cut in places that I knew wouldn't kill me: my shoulder, my forearm, my triceps, places I could conceal with clothes so as not to draw any unwanted attention to myself. Sir's flaccid member stiffened the more his eyes lingered on the jagged lines of abused flesh.

"That's very nice, Fido."

Sir, pet ...

"It's the unsavory aspects of lust that allow sex to be more pleasurable—the more unsavory it is, the more delicious."

"Tell me more, Sir," I whispered.

"I want to own a young boy like you. I'd like to slice off all four of your limbs and cauterize them with hot coal. I won't cut the limbs too close to the torso, as I do not want to kill you. I'd keep you well fed and fuck your torso. A living Fleshlight to use at my behest."

That's all? I've heard worse, man. Come on, surprise me.

"Yes, Sir, what else would you like to do to me?"

"Do you like what you hear?"

"Here's the proof ..."

I pulled down my boxers, exposing my erection to him.

"I'd like to cornhole you right where you shit."

"Would you?"

I turned around and spread my ass cheeks at the camera. He surely had to wonder how I manage to keep my shit from just falling out.

"I want you to squat on top of me as I suck a nice, wet clot of shit out of your guts," he said, stroking his cock even faster. "I want to smear a drug all over you that makes you itchy. I want you to be so itchy you're unable to stop scratching yourself. You scratch yourself raw. You scratch yourself until you bleed. You scrape patches of skin off your face ... your chest ... your ass."

He pauses in between words as he rasps. He beats his meat so hard that a slapping sound bounces off his walls.

"Your asshole ... fuck, it's so ruined. I bet you let your daddy fuck you in it. I bet he was your first fuck. I bet he threw you to all his sick friends and let them take turns gut-fucking you raw. You like that, huh? The thought of your daddy barebacking you like the little cum breeder you are?"

"Yes, Sir. He did."

"Fuck ..."

"What else would you do to me if I was there with you?"

"I would break your fingers one by one. Crack 'em backwards like they're twigs. I would slice you open from your sternum and pull out your guts. Your innards would land on hot coal and cook in front of you. I would then feast on them as you watched."

"And?"

"I'll drive a flaming nail into each of your eyes, into each of your nipples, into your asshole ... Fuck ... I'd burn you from the inside out. "

"Any requests?"

"I want to see blood. Cut yourself for Daddy, pet."

I opened up the drawer of my desk and pulled out my boxcutter. I thumbed the blade out and touched the tip with my finger; a halfhearted press drew a bead of crimson. I placed the tip of the blade against my wrist and peeled under a hard layer of scar tissue, cutting into thick rubber. I drew down another line of red, cutting into lumps that looked like dried papier mâché. Dark blood sluiced my flesh. I smeared the blood on my hand and used it to stroke my cock.

"Mmm, tell me more, Daddy," I rasped.

"I'd like to see you ingest horse medicine and watch you violently shit your bleeding guts out. I want to see your asshole dilate as the medicine burns you from the inside ... blood and hot shit spew out as ... fuck ..."

"F-fuck yes," I groaned, pumping myself as my climax descended on me. A trail of blood and semen slid down my gut.

After a few moments, he cleared his throat. "Thank you, pet."

"Don't mention it."

"I'm sorry."

"Don't be."

"I wish I was dead."

A notification of the promised payment popped up on the top right of my screen. I knew I could leave now, yet a glint of curiosity lingered in the back of my head.

"Why do you wish you were dead?" I asked.

"I'm sick."

"Can't you go to the hospital and get that checked out? I don't see why—"

"There's nothing any hospital can do to cure what I have," he hissed, cutting me off. "It's in my blood—it lives inside me, and it will die with me. Tell me, if you do everything right and still have everything turn out wrong, then what's the point?"

"What happened?"

"Nobody ever talks about how time slows down when you're glum, how each minute becomes excruciating when it hurts to be alive, only to have nothing to live for."

"I hate that word," I said.

"Which one?"

"Glum."

"How come?"

"Because."

"Tell me, pet."

"It's a depression that pisses other people off. It's an aggressive type of sadness that rubs other people the wrong way."

"I see."

"Would you like me to stay on a little longer?"

"That won't be necessary. I've been looking into your eyes; the same sickness inside me is inside you. I know you feel it."

"What does it feel like?"

"It feels like boredom. Like constantly chasing a fleeting high that never truly satisfies you. Like scratching an itch that never stops. There's no name for it. All I know is that every waking moment of your life is dark. It's a darkness so heavy it taints even your happiest memories. You look back and try to seek solace in a memory in your life where things were good ... only to realize that everything is filthy. You expect the world to step gingerly around you because of how broken you feel. You hope others are careful to not break you any more than you already are, but they never are. Not for people like us, the sick ones. No. There's no sympathy. No kindness. Your life is already over. All you're doing is kicking the can further down the road."

A sharp bite of pain nipped at me as I realized I'd unconsciously dug my nails into the bed of my palm. A massive boulder pushed down on my chest.

"I don't know what you're talking about."

"Oh, but you do. You know it's easier for everyone else to see us as monsters. It makes them feel safe; they don't need to think about us as people. To everyone else, we're nothing."

His window suddenly closed on the browser. I took that as my cue to sign off.

My phone rang.

"Novak."

"Did you get me my money, Dane?"

"I got you your money all right. I hope he's not a usual because I may have over-charged."

"What he doesn't know won't kill him. Wire it to me, kid."

"On it."

"I've got another guy who wants you to entertain him in about an hour. I'll send the link to you now. Don't be late."

He hung up.

I ambled to the bathroom and tore open the medicine cabinet. Bottles of prescription pills (that I totally didn't have a prescription for, thanks, Novak) stared at me. I reached for one at random and dry swallowed a couple.

Maybe I'll just pass on this next client. Sorry, Novak.

~

I exited the elevator and walked out into the street. My mind ripped between what I saw and what I was trying to feel: something, anything. Echoes of lost memories laughed from the corner of my eyes, taunting me. *I am not human; I am a shell of what I am wanting to forget. My mind is a fog of silence and screams.*

I need some air.

~

Cars lined the road down the block; I strolled down the pavement. Rats scurried about the heaps of trash and used syringes. The curb was lined with cigarette butts and human feces. My nose caught a drop of rain, signaling a light drizzle. Thunder loomed in the distance as the shower cascaded into a stream from the midnight blue. The patter on the concrete captured the rhythms of a sleeping street. Ripples bounced and spattered in pools formed by the cracks in the pavement. I stared back down the road, staring at the night sky through naked steel skeletons and angular fragments of bare cement.

Ahead, a sign blazed in sickly amber neon: COLD BEER HERE. Music rumbled in the air, rising and falling as doors opened and closed.

A smoking bar.

I stepped inside.

Garth Brooks thrummed on the jukebox as I twirled on the rickety barstool. A pint of Budweiser and a black ashtray sat in front of me. The tip of my Marlboro soaked up the flame of my match. I sucked in a long, hard drag. A neon cigarette sign hung above the bar, tinting the smoke a shade of twilight indigo. Bar pool balls clicked and clacked to the tune of the low chatter of the bar's sparse patrons.

I'd always been partial to booze as lubrication, a layer of protection from the demons in my head. Clear-eyed sobriety was for the cured people. This was where I went when I needed to forget, when I needed to watch other drunk zombies and invent stories about them in my head.

For instance, take the guy across the bar. His ashen beard wears a thick coat of beer foam. He's in a flannel shirt, his jeans are ripped, and his beer belly protrudes from his grease-stained white undershirt. On the shirt is the logo of the Eagles. He's got no job, but he sure does pat himself on the back for his good taste in music. His kids probably hate him for being a fat, useless lush. His wife cheats on him because of how he's let his body go. She regrets marrying him and wishes she could undo the past twenty years. Maybe you should've gone with the guy your parents liked, toots. Too late now. The tattoos covering this chubster's neck probably weren't there when he proposed to her. I suppose he dressed to impress, swooned the in-laws before getting comfortable and showing her who he was: a nobody. An overweight sack of nothing.

I kept an eye on the door as people on the street came and went one after the other. The next part of my plan was dependent on who came in alone. I started on my third pint as a tall brunette sauntered in.

Joe?

He looked like the kind of man Joe would've grown up to be—tall, handsome, sturdy. His strut exuded an air of confidence someone would have if they'd grown up with their praises sung. I decided he would do. I hadn't seen Joe since he was a teenager, so I couldn't be too sure he even still looked the same. I'd been chasing him all my life, desperate, hopeless.

The man's gaze lingered more on the scattering of men in the place than the women.

He parked two seats away from me and ordered a Budweiser. His accent told me he wasn't from these parts. He paid out of his pocket—no wallet, no briefcase. It was clear this guy was here for the singular purpose of getting shitfaced. I took a swig of my beer as he scanned the room. Our eyes crossed paths several times but not long enough to rouse suspicion.

I carried my empty glass over to the seat next to him and set it down on the bar. The bartender took this as his cue to fill 'er up. The man's drink was empty too. He met me with a cursory glance before flagging down the bartender.

"I'll have a refill too, please." He turned his seat to mine, a grin plastered on his face.

I wondered why someone as handsome as him was alone at a local dive bar on a weeknight. *Does he have a girlfriend? What does he do to pay for the insanely expensive rent in a city like this? What does he do to afford the cost of mere existence?* There was a yawning pause between the sip he took of his fresh pint and what he eventually asked.

"Are you old enough to be here, boy?"

Boy. Every time.

"I'm old enough to do a lot of things."

"You don't look a day over seventeen. How old are you?"

"Definitely not seventeen. But, in your defense, I do get carded now and then."

"I see."

"I couldn't help but notice your accent; where in the UK are you from?"

"Ah. Liverpool. Whereabouts are you from?"

"Nowhere."

"Is that back west?" he asked, scoffing up a mild laugh.

"I'm from nowhere, and I'm heading nowhere fast."

"I hope you don't mind me being curt, but what's a beautiful thing like you doing in a place like this tonight?"

Beautiful. He must be really fucking drunk.

"Hoping someone like you would talk to me, I guess."

"Well then."

There was always something off-putting about a man who would want to be with someone who looked as young as me, but I digress. I soaked in his wolfish grin.

I hadn't taken a guy home since Novak got me that apartment. I was bored, he was down to fuck, he was wired, and I seized the opportunity. His name was

Derek, not Joe. And Novak? Well, what he didn't know wouldn't hurt him.

Derek was 32 and worked in real estate development. On the way back, he told me his life story; I pretended to be interested. It was what I did, convinced people that they were the most special thing in the fucking world, that the sun shined out of their ass. His sales pitch about how great he was, was far more interesting to him than it was to me.

"So this is what you do to avoid STDs?" he asked, nodding at my desktop with the Chaturbate page glowing.

I didn't laugh. *He thinks this desktop and ring light is out there? He doesn't know half of it.* I was bored, so I decided to oblige him. "Sometimes, when I think of how I've arrived at the point that the thing I worry about most in life is avoiding STDs, I don't know whether I should be happy or cry."

"It must be nice not having a boss. I can't stand mine. People don't quit bad jobs; they quit bad bosses."

"I do have a boss. Friend of my dad's. Water?"

"Sure."

I thought his good looks would fade after we both sobered up. No sir, this one was a looker. Light blue eyes, tanned skin, thick brown hair, and all.

A glimpse of myself stared back at me in the mirror as I made my way back to Derek. Smudged eyeliner, tousled ice blond hair, black chipped nail polish ... My faded Led Zeppelin shirt was torn at the collar, and my ripped skinny jeans did little to make me look presentable.

I handed the glass to him.

"Thanks."

I sat down, leaned back, and lit up a cigarette.

"So, what do you do specifically?" He nodded his head at my desktop.

"I sell my time and kill my body."

He took a slow sip of water, all the while holding my gaze. He placed a hand on my inner thigh and leaned in.

"I see ..."

"What else do you do besides real estate?"

"I'm still in school. Getting my master's in business, working on the side. You?"

I took a deep breath.

"I was an awful student in high school. But, let's just say that the *education* I had wasn't really necessary for what I do."

"Uh, uh." He nodded, his eyebrow raised.

"Anway, school wasn't doing it for me, and neither was my home. So I left. I had no resume, so I had to use what I had. I doubt I'd need to spell it out for you.

Hitchhiking and crumby motels that didn't ask for IDs. Older men who'd say I was their nephew. There are loopholes around anything where degeneracy is concerned."

"I could've sworn you were still in school."

"What can I say? Shaving ages me down at least three years."

"So you're twenty?"

"Am I?"

"Tell me more."

I thought about why I took Derek home. Was it because I wanted to be in control this time? Did I want to test Novak and see what would happen? Maybe I just want to feel *something*. Anything. Maybe I wanted to know what intimacy felt like. What sex felt like without the transaction.

(The word intimacy—all eight letters—fascinated me. It's a word with a slight hiss to it. It's a need, a raw, empty need to be satisfied, something that refuses to be ignored, like a child you have to raise. What can you do? It's yours.)

Maybe I just wanted to confide in a stranger and see what his reaction was. Maybe all the cliches about talking to someone would provide the necessary release. Anyone burdened with a secret itched to tell it. Maybe he, too, had the sickness.

I cracked my knuckles, then my neck. "So, where should I begin?"

"From the start."

Derek shifted forward and lay on his stomach, propping his head up with both his hands in a tell-me-a-story kind of way.

"Feel free to pause me at any time if you happen to get bored," I said, though I doubted anyone who'd never met a hooker-turned-webcam-model would find any of it dull.

He nodded.

"I left school in the middle of Junior year because of some shit going on at home. My parents had just gotten a divorce, and since most fathers tend to get screwed over as far as custody is concerned, I was stuck living with mother dearest, who, for all intents and purposes, was never dear to me ..."

I trailed off and took a seat in a chair next to the nightstand, lighting another cigarette.

"So, all the shit about people turning gay because of an absentee father and overbearing mother is true," Derek said in jest.

This earned him a chuckle.

"I can't speak for anyone else, but I wouldn't call her overbearing. I will, however, call her a cunt. My last interaction with her was when I texted her a selfie of me with a client's cum all over my face. I blocked her number after sending it. I sincerely hope she saw it."

This made his eyes widen. Unflappable Derek was gone.

"I can almost guarantee you it's a way more interesting story than mine," Derek said.

I laughed and took a nice long drag.

"So, I'd never hitchhiked before, but I did know how to win the favors of older men. Daddy taught me well. I dumped a bunch of shit into my backpack and walked for a couple of hours to the first busy street. I held my thumb up and counted the cars and trucks zipping by. Some old fuck eventually pulled over. It looked like he was in his late fifties."

"Don't tell me you ..."

"You bet I did. He pretended to be my dad. He called me son and asked me to call him daddy. He stuck his cock in my mouth while I played with his balls. Thanks to some practice I'd had, I managed to deepthroat him and get him to cum in under a minute. I lapped up the salty taste of him as he squirted down the back of my throat, then I sat on his face while he tongued my asshole. He licked and sucked my grubby ass as I came on his chest."

Derek looked at me aghast. "And does this person you had practiced on happen to be a married man with kids who saw you on the side?"

"Mhmm, pretty close, actually. He was a married man who was wed to my mother and whose ballsack I came from."

Derek swallowed loudly.

"I'm kidding," I chuckled.

"Fuck, you had me worried there for a second."

How precious.

"Shall I go on?"

"Please."

"Anyway, I made enough to hitchhike from motel to motel. Unfortunately, the ones that didn't care for ID were the ones that smelled like Tuesday night at a midwestern dive bar crapper. I'm talking smoke stains on the walls, the smell of piss in places that weren't limited to the bathrooms, and the sounds of women that were either getting fucked into a higher plane of existence or getting the shit kicked out of them. I never could tell the difference."

"This may sound like a stupid question, and I apologize in advance, but did he tell you his name?"

"Nah. I used to invent names for them in my head based on what they looked like, but I stopped when I lost count of them. To me, they were all John."

"Dare I ask?"

"Enough to get me an apartment in New York fucking City with no roommate."

Thanks, Novak. Couldn't have done it without ya.

"So, where was I? Oh, right. I started on this site called Flirt4Free. I would hop on using the pixelated front camera of my phone, which was made worse by the dim lighting in my room. I will admit, although I've fucked a lot, I'd never actually seen myself naked from that angle. It took me a while to get hard because I was too caught up with how I looked. I didn't have enough to afford a gym membership because my finances relied on how many people railed me. My body was all cardio and zero commitment. That didn't matter; I found my audience. Turns out, old men who jack off to their stepsons aren't as rare as I thought. The money started coming in."

"So, like, I don't know how to ask this, but what did you do?" he asked, taking a long sip of water.

"I smiled and called them *daddy*," I said, mirroring him and bringing my glass to my lips.

"When was the last time you slept with a client?"

"Slept with." I smirked. "If only it were that easy. Nah, I was with this guy about a week ago. He's a regular of mine who likes to pretend to be my doctor. Prostate and dick exams, all that jazz. It was kind of different this time, though, because he wanted me to inspect him."

I left out the part where I saw someone die in front of me as soon as I got out of the session.

"Anyways, after a couple of months, my online clientele began to dry up, so Dad's friend started sending me to other sites. I found one called Chaturbate, which had more users watching. This helped me grow my Boy Lolita brand. Flirt4free took 75% of my earnings, and Chaturbate took only about 20%. You live and learn."

"Do you hop on—sorry, what was it again?—whenever you need some extra cash?" he asked.

"Chaturbate," I said. "Man, I wish it was that easy, hopping on only whenever I needed groceries. If only the algorithm was that friendly. I work five days a week, and each session lasts about four hours. Equipment is everything. Yes, some desperate fucks will watch you regardless, so long as you're vaguely attractive or look like someone from their lives they'd like to fuck. It's not uncommon that I've had to read off a script and use the name of one of their sons or nephews."

"What kind of stuff do you do online?"

"I think I've had enough of this talk."

"No, no. I'm interested. Please."

His enthusiasm was pitiful. He talked like he was under the impression he was doing me a favor, like I was better than I was yesterday because I was now in his glorious presence.

I was bored and decided it was time for some fun.

"Okay, then."

I pulled my shirt over my head and watched as his jaw slackened.

"Like what you see?"

"What—what happened? Did you? Did someone do that to you?"

"You asked what kind of stuff I did online. I don't just jack off for them; I do this too."

"That ... that shit's allowed on Chaturbate?"

"Nah. I have a special site for these clients. They pay much more. Ever heard of the dark web? Red rooms and such?"

"The dark what?"

"In addition to getting myself off, this is how I help them get off."

"H-how do you mean?"

"How much time do you have?"

"As much as you're willing to give me."

I nodded several times and took a deep, filling breath.

"I made my first cut when I was about thirteen. Since then, I'd been doing it quite frequently; slicing, dicing, carving, and burning. It's how I coped with being raped, fist fucked, beaten, and made to swallow every by-product produced by the human body.

"The first word I dug into myself was *ANIMAL*. I used a random kitchen knife to do it. The first cut was a diagonal line; the next one was the same. The word *ANIMAL* is written in horizontal and vertical lines; that made the incisions easy. It was like the word existed beneath my skin and cutting it out released me of it. That was how it was since then; my mind screamed, and I released it of its pain. Except I started making money off letting people watch."

"I don't get it. I don't see how hurting yourself could make you feel better."

"You know how some people tell you they have to hurt because without pain, all they'll have is numbness?"

"Y-yeah, I suppose."

"What if it's not like that at all?" I leaned in closer to him. "What if some people seek out pain because it can feel good? What if, to some people, the pain feels like the hands of a lover exploring you for the first time?"

Our foreheads touched as the tip of his nose brushed against mine. A tingle rose up my leg as his fingers traced the scars behind my right shoulder blade. The warmth of his exhale was like the first glimpse of sunlight after a year-long monsoon.

"How about I just show you what I do."

"S-sure."

"Chaturbate and Flirt4free are one thing, but I get most of my money from this other site."

"What's it called?"

"Let's just say you can't access it if you simply paste the URL into a standard search engine."

I fired up the TOR software to hack into its browser.

He chuckled and leaned back on both his palms. "So the dark web isn't just this conspiracy theory?"

"Nope, it's right here," I said, nodding toward the screen.

"What am I looking at?"

"The place where all the freaks are: The Red Den. You can find some of the sickest shit on here. What I offer doesn't have as much demand, but if you can attract as much as one client for an hour, you're guaranteed to make bank."

"Fuck, Dane."

I slid onto the bed and moved behind him, massaging his shoulders.

"What kind of shit can you find on the dark web? I thought it was just a place where people could buy drugs and guns and shit."

I leaned in next to his ear. "You can find all kinds of things. Looking through it like I have is a frank reminder that we're all just made of meat. That and some people have weird hobbies."

"What kind of hobbies?"

"Ever heard of hurtcore?"

"Can't say I have."

"I actually starred in one as a kid. They're videos of people raping and torturing children. Inflicting pain so bad that the kid sometimes dies. Some communities have about ten thousand online members at a time. To get into these pages, you have to submit your own video. Aspiring members are encouraged to film their kids or students. It's sick stuff."

"That's fucking disgusting."

"It is," I said, lighting another cigarette. "Have you ever heard of smashing videos?"

"Smashing?"

"Yeah. It's when you stomp on helpless animals until they're a bloody pulp."

"No, and I'm quite glad I haven't."

"I saw this one video of a guy holding a little Asian girl at gunpoint and forcing her to step on these hamsters. She was crying and screaming the entire time; it excited him. He zoomed in on their eyes popping out and their guts squirting out of their ass. He then took the entrails and rubbed them on her face as he jerked off on her. Apparently, hurting kids isn't the only weird hobby these hurtcore freaks like."

"And you watched this why?"

"Because. Look, when I was setting up my page, I searched up a couple of videos to see what I'd be competing with. I saw someone nail a kitten to the floor and cut off its limbs with a box cutter. He put it in a ziplock bag and videoed its face as it died. I saw this other one where a dog was fucked in the ass with a drill. Its bloody guts were still attached to the drill bit when he yanked it—"

"I don't know how much more of this I can listen to," Derek said, cutting me off.

"Damn. I was just about to tell you about the cartel killings. I should probably end this discussion on a lighter note."

He raises an eyebrow. "There's a lighter note?"

"Well, I once saw a video of a pitbull chewing a guy's junk off. It was still attached to him like cheese on a hot pizza. The guy deserved it, though. He was a rapist piece of shit."

"Well then." He snickered. "You don't do any of that stuff, do you?"

"I do. Though, not all fetishes involve outright murder. Some people just want to see sick shit. That's where I come in."

"I'd like to see one of them."

"All right. Take off your shirt."

"Now?" Derek said, getting up to put his drink on the nightstand.

"Now, Derek."

He propped himself up and pulled his shirt off. My eyes lingered on his tanned skin and the smattering of hair dusting his brawny chest and abs. In the dim lighting of my bedroom, his light eyes drowned me in their azure depth.

I guided his eyes to the screen as the video finished buffering. I was in the same spot he and I sat in now. In the center of the dark room, lit by an amateur ring light, sat me. I wore nothing but a jockstrap. I rose to my knees, reached for something offscreen, and held it into focus.

It was a policeman baton. I licked down the shaft like I was getting someone's cock primed for a good suck. I then propped the baton up and stood above it as I got into a squat and let the black metal sink into me.

"Why so tense? We haven't even gotten started."

Derek's crotch twitched under my touch.

I grazed my teeth up along his cheek and made my way to his earlobe, giving it a soft nibble. He shuddered as his hand moved, resting just above the button of his jeans. I slid my hand down his forearm and met his palm with mine. My hand rested right below the area of his happy trail. He tilted his head back as I marked a trail of kisses down his neck.

"You're definitely not a shy one," he said, gripping my hand and lowering it to the swell in his jeans. His dick stiffened in my grasp.

He looked back at the screen. In it, I was stroking myself. I'd slipped a leather blindfold on and linked handcuffs around my wrists. A ball gag was strapped to my mouth. My heart raced from the sheer thrill of it; having a live audience to my degradation was far more exciting than anonymous avatars on the internet.

I wet my lips and sucked on his neck.

He reached back, gripped the back of my head, and brought my mouth to his. I kissed him, hard.

"I really need to take care of this. Give me a hand?"

Wasting no time, I shoved my hand into his waistband and found his warm shaft. I teased him a little beneath his shorts and used my other hand to direct his head back to the monitor. On the screen, my back was now facing the camera as I brandished a flogger. Derek winced as the flogger cracked down on my back. Red welts formed down my flesh as the leather bit into me.

I reached into his briefs and freed his cock. My heart slammed into my chest at the sight of him. His erection curved slightly to the side; it was thick, veiny, and stuck out through a thick patch of pubic hair. The tip reddened as I moved my hand down the shaft; my thumb slid over the pearl of moisture forming in his slit. Derek slumped back on my chest as I quickened my strokes, using his warm skin as friction on my throbbing erection. My other hand tweaked his pebbled nipple, stimulating him evenly. I may not have been stroking my cock, but stroking his as he watched me turned me on even more. His breathing deepened; the sound of him on the edge shot a bolt of intensity down my spine.

His body tensed up.

In the video, I was laying down; my asshole faced the camera as I pulled out the baton. The base of my gaping anus undulated like a dog's yawning maw. My ass cheeks were blackened with bruises from beatings I'd given myself.

From inside the box, I extracted a speculum and inserted it into my gaping anus, prying it open to expose the pink musculature of my soggy, elastic cavity. You could make out every jellied crease of my used rectal cavern.

My next excavation into the black box of mysteries gave me a jar of earth. Inside the jar was my collection of maggots, each the gray shade of stillborn infants. I scooped up a handful and plunged them into my sodden rectum. They crawled and slithered inside me, nuzzling against my prostate as my mud-caked fist beat my cock. The microphone picked up every squelching waterlogged noise.

Derek sat in awe, absorbing the sights and sounds like a lobotomized witness at a car crash.

My sheathed cock rubbed against Derek's back, eliciting a delightful pulse from the pressure.

The screen zoomed into me closer now as I emptied the contents of the black box. Inside it was a collection of metal tools used to break skin: razor blades, scalpels, syringes, pins, needles ... the like.

"Ummm, I don't know about this," he said. His tone wavered with uncertainty, yet his erection yielded to no such protests.

"This may sound a bit on-the-nose, so forgive me in advance, but we've gotten to the climax."

He nodded.

A blanket of awareness settled over us. I reached into the nightstand and pulled out a small blade. I held it toward the light, just in front of his face. His eyes widened slightly. My strokes resumed as he sucked in a sharp breath

"Do you trust me?"

"Yeah."

His lips tightened as he swallowed back a large gulp. His eyes flicked back to the screen.

On the screen, the mucky maggot gruel splatted beneath me. I fished the rest out, fitting all five fingers inside my cavity. I squeezed the worms in my fist, and they ruptured in fat bulbs of juice. I sucked the mucoid matter into my mouth and mashed it around with my tongue. Gray discharge oozed out of my gums as I chewed the slithering babies.

Then I took a razor blade and made light cuts on the soft, scarred tissue of my inner thighs and pubic mound. Blood dripped onto my cock, and I stroked my length with the blood as a lubricant.

Derek's eyes locked on the screen as light spots of blood and pus coagulated in pink, foamy hills.

"Fuck ..." he rasped.

I shifted position to being on my knees at the foot of the bed. Wet with spit, my hand hastened its stroking of Derek's cock. The bottom of my wrist grazed the end of his brown bushel of pubic hair. My pulse slammed in my ears as my heart thumped like a rabbit's foot. Doing *this* to myself had lost its fun. Doing it to someone else was exhilarating. The rapidness of his breathing told me how close he was to meeting his climax.

His cheeks were flushed. His chest was littered with large red patches. Adrenaline surged through my veins. I knelt down in front of him as I pumped him faster. Desire coursed through me like a savage song from a violin slicing through air particles. My erection pressed painfully against my underwear.

My moist lips found the salty tip of his cock as I pumped his shaft up and down to the hilt.

"Yes," he whimpered. "Just like ... fuck ... fuck!"

I trailed my tongue up and down the length of him, then took him deeper in my mouth again and again, slightly grazing the back of his fleshy stem with my teeth. I gave the base of his cock a tight squeeze and lapped up the salty moisture from his slit. His hips rocked upward as primal moans seethed through his gritted teeth.

His hand found the back of my head. He gripped a fistful of my hair and shoved me down with determined force. The spear of savory flesh raked down the back of my throat, evoking wet gags. I matched his force with my fingers and plunged two dry fingers up his ass.

"Ow, fuck!" he yipped.

I didn't hear the word *stop*.

I kept going, violating his flesh with my spiderlike digits as he power-fucked my mouth. *Yes, fuck me. Violate me. Use me. I am your fucktoy and nothing more.*

"Fuck ..." A gagged gurgle involuntarily left his lips "I'm so fucking close."

He tightened his grip on my hair, practically tearing it from the roots like a handful of petulant weeds. His leg muscles tensed as my nail dug into the inside of his rectum. The blade in my other hand sliced a straight line in his inner thigh.

On the screen, I picked up the knife, pressed it against my neck, and slit my throat. A scarlet flood sprayed out onto the floor and spilled down to my chest, coating my entire body in dark crimson.

Derek heaved forward as I thrusted my head down to his pubis, swallowing the entire length of him as his release welled at the back of my throat.

He shuddered as I swallowed every last drop of him, teasing him in his heightened state of sensitivity.

"Fuck ... this," he rasped, his face contorted in revulsion.

He cocked his arm back. I knew what was coming, but I couldn't compel myself to move. He slapped me so hard my tooth bit into my cheek. He shoved me to the side, buttoned up his pants, and grabbed his shirt. He stumbled for the door and turned to face me.

"You're a sick fuck, you know that? You're a disgusting sick fuck!"

Fresh blood eased down the corner of my mouth. A smile crept up my face as I blew him a kiss. He flashed me one last look of disgust and then slammed the door behind him.

I didn't need the sex; I didn't need to come either. I just needed to bear witness to the scandal and fear in someone's eyes as innocence was violated. I wanted to see a normal person introduced to this so-called sickness. This feeling of being the corruptor was new—exhilarating. I'd let people burn me, shit on me, piss in my eyes, and defecate wet bowel sludge down my throat. They've cut my flesh, pumped me full of drugs, and used me as a punching bag. I'd seen and felt it all.

The only thing that truly scared me, though, at this point, was how tedious it had all become to me. The entire world was in this city, and I'd seen the entire world. The entire world had had its way with me. The world fucked me the day I was born and continued to fuck me every day after. Perhaps we all had fragments of the sickness to some degree. Maybe no one was immune to it—some people were just better at hiding it than others.

My phone buzzed.

"Novak."

"You're testing me, kid."

"Hey, I made you nine thousand bucks earlier. So what if I missed one client?"

"And you think that's enough to cover everything? You want me to start pimping your ass out to some of the more hardcore clients? I know a guy who has an amputee kink. This fucker just so happens to have a friend who's in the market for a human Fleshlight. Just say the word."

"Hey, come on, man. I needed a break."

"Sure, I'll give you a break. Just let one of my guys turn your arms and legs into stumps while fucking ya; that'll give you enough to take a month off. We got a deal, kid?"

"No. Look, I'm sorry. I'll—"

"Sorry don't cut it. You're mine; you hear me? Don't make me come by and remind you."

He hung up. I didn't know how much longer I could keep doing this. My eyes flitted to the book I purchased about a week ago: a hardboiled detective drama. The corner of my eyes caught it a few weeks ago in a bookstore window as I walked through the city. Its author was hosting a book signing the next day.

CHAPTER 16 : SUMMER OF 2019

I tore down Second Avenue, hoping my shoes would stay intact; these New York streets were not made for clean shoes (or running). The thick August air sank its humidity into my clothes. My armpits were drenched in sweat. I inwardly thanked myself for wearing black.

I finally reached the venue—a chic bookstore that looked like some sort of place where high-end art exhibits were held. It was a studio of unpainted cement and massive glass doors, completely desaturated and limited to various hues of white and gray. Very hipster.

Anticipation shortened my breath as I forced thoughts of the possibility of failure out of my mind. I didn't care if I had to tear this entire building down myself; I was going to see him, and he would remember me.

He had to.

I took stock of myself and patted my hair, hastily flattening all the stray strands that had been ravaged by the windy streets. I straightened up my button-down shirt and wiped debris from my jeans. I hadn't thought about what to wear, so I opted for a black button-down shirt to conceal as much of me as possible and I dabbed concealer on my chin to hide the scars from old cold sores.

This'll have to do.

The cold air instantly chilled me as I walked through the front door. The lobby was dimly lit from up above, and the air conditioners were on full blast. *Outlast it and just defrost outside later,* I told myself.

Approaching the ticket guy, I scanned the room to see if I could catch a glimpse of Joe somewhere. To my relief, everyone else seemed to be clad in a similar semi-casual motif.

"Twenty-five bucks," the attendant said, looking at me like I was someone's lost kid.

I fumbled in my pocket for my wallet as nausea roiled through my gut at the thought of already looking like an idiot. The damned wallet was stuck in my abnormally compressed jeans. I took a deep breath, steadying myself, and slowly inserted two fingers to pry out the worn leather. My panic subsided as I handed him the money.

"Enjoy the book signing," he said with no smile as he attended to the next person.

Further into the venue, I found an empty seat somewhere near the back. The paranoia lingered in the recesses of my mind like toxins aching to spread loose from the confines of a viper's bite. Here I was, about to see my childhood best friend that I had not seen in just under two decades, someone whose house I had practically lived in. Someone who I'd been chasing ever since. Someone who I had spent almost every moment of free time with, who promised me we would be friends forever. Someone who happened to be my first kiss. Waves of anticipation expanded, gurgling in my bowels. And now I wanted to turn back and sprint all the way back to my apartment.

The room closed in on me as talons of disquietude flanked the edge of my consciousness. I chewed my upper lip like meat. I thrived on intensity, but this vile combination of consternation and exhaustion had the inverse sensation. Worried thoughts metastasized in my head: the thought of being rejected, the emptiness of a life without ever—

The lights dimmed.

Leave. He wants nothing to do with you. He never did. It was all in your head. A voice at the back of my head buzzed like a gnat, burrowing and whispering with venom.

"Ladies and gentlemen, if I could have your attention, please," a woman said before proceeding to prattle on incessantly, then, "... and the author of *Headhunter*, Joseph Schilling." Maybe his parents had split up too; I hope it wasn't as messy as mine.

And there he was.

Joe walked up to the microphone in the center of the room. All conversation had suddenly ceased. The photo on the dust jacket didn't do him justice; he was absolutely stunning in person. He was taller than I expected, yet he radiated gentle control. His thick hair still had those luscious waves, and he'd lost all his baby fat. His wardrobe was humble yet expensive, paradoxical just like everything about him.

After a brief opening monologue about why he wrote the book—a book he wrote because he was fascinated with cold cases and mysteries—the interviewer opened the floor to questions.

I didn't raise my hand.

Joe answered several of them. The deep cadence of his voice hummed in my head, yet I did not *hear* anything he said. I sat there enraptured by his every pause, his every lilt, the way each word curled off his tongue, the clarity with which he spoke, the way he crooned certain words … and just like that, summer of 2004 rushed back to me.

He paused for a moment, snapping me back into the present. His eyes locked on mine. He and I were frozen in time. And I swore, at that moment, his shocked expression turned into an inscrutable grin … just before he called on the middle-aged man at the other end of the room.

My heart sank in my chest. What did I expect? That he'd care to talk to me after all this time? This beautiful man with a booming career, a loving fiancé, a happy future … What the hell would he want with me?

"Fuck it," I muttered under my breath.

When the event ended, I jumped off my seat and beelined toward the exit. I didn't stay for drinks; I didn't care. Or maybe I cared too much. Either way, I trudged through the thoughts and forced myself to move. I took one last look at Joe, accepting the fact that my time with him was fun but that I'd never see him again. I took one fleeting look back and saw him animatedly describing something with large hand gestures as he lost himself in a conversation. The man towered over him, and the woman was in full glamor, yet he had complete control of both the conversation and their attention ... All while I stood there, shaking like a shaved cat.

He turned his head and looked right at me like he had just seen something in the air. At that moment, it felt like the air in the room had dried up; my soft clothes felt like scabs. The glint in his eyes had me standing atop a windswept cliff at the edge of the world. A roar of the waves on the shore below me crashed and boomed. I took a fleeting step toward him, but his expression stiffened and his eyes passed over me. His contemptuous dismissal left me with smoldering disappointment.

I just wanted out.

Anywhere was better than here. Even the chaos of the street I lived on; the carjackings, murders, rapes, the constant defilement of the creatures of the polluted night. The city was a fortress of skyscrapers cloaked in lights and colors concealing a freshly gang-raped streetwalker weeping on the piss- and shit-stained concrete of the sidewalk.

I spun around and ambled out onto the street, lighting a cigarette and cursing myself for my vicious egotism. I took a massive drag and sucked as much nicotine as I could into my lungs, taking in the smoker's high. I tucked another smoke behind my ear—one certainly wouldn't be enough. I planned to skip the closest subway entrance and walk down a couple of blocks to the next one. I was going to need some time to look up at the sky as I sank into the crowded sea of strangers at the crosswalk.

"Sir, wait!" someone yelled, his voice a moist rattle of phlegm scraping against his throat.

It was the man who sold me the ticket. He was winded, pausing to catch his breath. *What could he want?* I thought to myself. A line of people had queued in front of the signing table to purchase the book, something I had no intention of doing. I already had a copy in my backpack. I doubted Joe was chasing everyone down in a desperate attempt to give every last one of them his autograph. So ... why?

"Yes?" was all I could say.

"I'm sorry to bother you, but are you Dane? Dane ... Chan ..."

"Chandler. Dane Chandler."

"Yes! Ummm, yeah, I don't exactly know how to tell you this, but Mr. Schilling would like to meet you."

I was at a standstill, unable to process what he had just said. Of all the imagined stories in my mind, I did not expect this. Hell, I lost all hope that he even remembered my name. Nerves from the days of my childhood resurfaced and boiled to a fever pitch.

"Sir?" he said, impatient now.

"I'm sorry ..." I had half the mind to tell him he was mistaken. Fuck it. "I'll head back with you," I said with a spiritless sigh. I followed behind him as we made our way back to the bookstore. The attendant wove us through the crowd, guiding me like I was a lost child. My stomach was in shambles, brewing like it was filled with muriatic acid.

"So, how do you know Joe?"

"We were friends as kids. I haven't seen him in over fifteen years, though." *It's crazy to think about how much time it's been since then.*

"So why didn't you say hi? Joe's one of the friendliest people I've ever met. I'm sure he'll be ecstatic to see you. Heck, he was pretty excited when he told me to go after you." He playfully nudged me.

He escorted me back into the room. The temperature felt warmer due to all the people in the room. I had the sudden urge to throw up. Fear and anticipation mingled in an unholy stew that swam through my bloodstream like an air bubble going straight for the heart.

There he was.

I forced a grin to conceal how cataclysmic an experience this was to me.

He was beautiful. Disarmingly so. His facial structure was still the same; my Joe. He was taller and more stacked, far more put together than I'd ever been.

He wore an expensive blazer that swelled at his biceps, opened to expose his light pink button-down, and khaki slacks with polished brown shoes. He wore the confident smile of someone who owned the room; smug, self-assured. But to me, he was Joe. He was Joe in the backyard, Joe from down the lane, and Joe who walked up to me as I was trying to catch crayfish by the creek ... the one who had asked me if I had any plans on "naming those crabs." I still chuckled at the thought of how this city boy was in such foreign territory in the rural suburbs.

"Have you figured out the difference between crayfish and crabs yet?" My voice cracked as I said this.

"Dane ..." He paused, utterly stupefied.

He didn't need to say anything anymore. He pulled me into the warmest hug I'd ever been given. His hand rubbed my back. He didn't know that I'd gladly stay like that until the day I perished.

"Suzie, Jeff, this is Dane."

"A pleasure," I said, extending to shake both their hands.

"How do you do?" Suzie said.

Joe took a step back, arms akimbo, and looked up, letting out a massive exhale. "Where the hell do I begin? Dane was ... I mean, *is* a dear friend of mine. I haven't seen him in years. I didn't even know he was coming," he said, flashing me a tender grin.

I produced a copy of his book from my shoulder bag and held it up to tell these people *I totally had a reason for coming here, I swear.*

"I was actually about to head out to dinner," Joe said. He spoke with the blithe manner of someone who had not a care in the world. His voice carried a sing-song, lilting baritone of a concert pianist knowing when to hit the next sublime note.

"My fiancé is busy, care to join?"

Fiancé.

"Oh my, we have to be at the airport early tomorrow. You two should go and catch up if it has been that long!" Jeff said.

"Dane?"

Awestruck, I muttered, "I think I'd like that."

"Well, that leaves just the two of us, I guess." Joe turned to me with a wink. "You hungry?"

"Starving."

"Well, what the hell are we waiting for? Know any good places around here?"

"Actually ... I don't get out much. And when I do, I normally treat myself to Dominos or something."

"Still a huge pizza guy, I see." Joe clapped my shoulder as he guided me to the exit.

I wanted to hold him. I wanted to pull him into another hug and never let him go. I wanted to tell him I refused to ever let him leave my sight. Loneliness had become so familiar that it had begun to feel like a friend, yet now the only real friend I'd ever had stood there. It was as if no time had passed since we'd last spoken.

"I didn't mean to show up out of the blue ... I just ..." I said impulsively. "I'm sorry."

Joe glanced sideways at me as if shocked I'd noticed something he was trying to hide. We walked out into the street; some people from the exhibits were hailing cabs.

"I tried to leave because I didn't want to startle you."

He stopped and shook his head, cutting me with a look of incredulity. Something was clearly on his mind because the lively and animated man Joe was just a few minutes before has been replaced by that shy child I knew all too well. Standing in his place was an exhausted wraith of a man, someone who had reached his quota of forced smiles and human interaction.

"No, Dane ..." he said with an air of reluctance. "It's not that I'm upset."

Everything around us, the entire street that was once bustling with the sounds of the city, went dead. Waiting for him to finish his thought was something akin to torture. We continued to walk forward, our steps grating against the pavement as I looked down, straining to not seek his gaze.

"Did you take a car here?" I said to cut through the quiet.

"Nah. Cassie has the car tonight. She had somewhere to be this evening. Between the two of us, I think she's beginning to get bored with all these book signings."

"Cassie?"

"Yes, my fiancé. Sorry ... it's just that I feel like no time has passed. It's like we're catching up from our last conversation. Dane, you look young enough to be one of my students."

Fiancé. The mere mention of it was like a sharp splinter being dug under my nail, the ache of loss.

"Looks like we have a lot of catching up to do."

"That's putting it mildly."

Joe held his hand up and signaled for a taxi. Coiling his finger was a tattoo of a cobra. Behind his hand in the sky was a thin moon veiled by an opaque gauze of city smog.

"Love your tattoo."

He chuckled, "Hah. Thanks; got it a while back. Cassie can't stand it, though. I'm glad you do."

It had been almost fifteen years and here he was, confiding in me as if we'd only been apart for a couple of days. All it took for all that time to evaporate was a few minutes with him. I grew anxious seeing how weary he looked. Was he going to take a rain check on dinner? Was he going to politely excuse himself and just leave me here? Was he going to make it impossible for me to ever see him again?

I can't lose him. Not tonight. Not again.

"Hey," I said, "there were a couple of restaurants and bars up ahead. Why don't we just try finding something up the street?"

"It's no problem, Dane, I'll just call an Uber ..." he said, floundering as he tried to locate his phone.

"No, no. I meant maybe we could just look for something to eat over here. It's starting to get busy a few blocks up. It'll take us about five minutes to find a place ..." I trailed off and stopped myself as I grasped for words in a strained effort to keep him here.

"Sure. I've never eaten here before."

A cloud of relief descended on me.

"It'll be an adventure, just like when we were kids."

That made him smile.

~

I didn't know what cruel trick of fate had befallen me, but I was next to Joe in a half-empty bar on a

Thursday night in New York City, a near decade and a half after he disappeared off the face of the earth.

We didn't choose this bar specifically, nor did either of us check online to assess its merit. I suppose the gravitational pull of the universe veered us to the one with the least people. The bar itself was dimly lit with deep blues and reds, very *Giallo*; you'd think we had stumbled onto the set of a Dario Argento film. A song I liked played on the speakers: "Apocalypse" by Cigarettes After Sex.

The table was narrow enough for us to speak without having to raise our voices. Joe was flanked by a scarlet and indigo glow like the moon of *Solaris*. All his prior confidence seemed to have dissipated. In its place was a slightly embarrassed smile.

He told me about himself, about Cassandra, about where he'd been all this time. He and his family had moved to Upstate Connecticut and settled there after his dad had gotten promoted to school principal. As for Joe, the beautiful autumn scenery in Connecticut was what he loved the most; he was only here for the book signing.

He asked me what I did for a living, making me choke on my Budweiser I told him I was self-employed and left it at that. If he ever visited my apartment, I'm sure he'd assume that the iMac desktop and webcam were for online client meetings. I asked him about what movies he'd seen recently. He told me he thought that *La La Land* was an overrated, overproduced musical—"It had white people explaining jazz to black people and unlikeable main characters ... and it glamorized late-stage capitalism and poverty in Los Angeles." I hadn't been to a movie theater in years, so I didn't have much to add to the conversation. Seeing his eyes light up as he talked about things he knew about was enough for me.

It turned out he'd been in and out of New York since 2014. All this time. I wondered if he and I were ever in the same vicinity. I wondered if he was beginning to suspect how anxious I was about sharing any parts of my life with him. Here he was going into immense detail about everything, and all I did was nod along. My throat thickened as a press of despair behind my eyes nearly forced warm tears down my cheeks.

He told me how little of our childhood together he remembered. I wanted to tell him that it was cruel of him to not say *goodbye*. Or that it was all that I wanted to remember. The two of us had been so distracted we'd barely even begun to cover the past that linked us both. What I needed was something concrete, a small memory of something to pick up and slip into this conversation for me to gently accost him and ask him why he never tried to contact me. I wanted to tell him how I'd never been the same since he left; how the feeling of having lost him put me in a state of grief that had rendered me emotionally catatonic, had made my chest feel like stones were surgically implanted into it.

But I just couldn't.

He told me about how his mom had been diagnosed with stomach cancer and had since gone into remission. Mrs. Jennings was perhaps the kindest and most beautiful woman I'd ever met, and the thought of her not existing was unendurable. The world was a brighter place by sheer virtue of her existence.

I was reminded of the way he could take a dark, sullen topic and deflate its seriousness with a humorous, offhand remark. He was an absolute charmer, still. I'd loved this man with every waking moment of my life, and I would continue to do so even if he no longer needed or wanted me.

His phone lit up with an incoming text, and I caught a glance at the time. It was past midnight. More people trickled into the venue.

"Fuck, I think this booze has gotten to me. I'm such a lightweight."

"Let's see, do you remember—"

"I'm sorry, I haven't been the most participative companion tonight," I said, cutting him off.

"Nonsense. Hey, Dane … I missed you."

I shook my head. "Then why didn't you call? Why didn't you write? Did you at least try?"

"I didn't. And I'm sorry."

The fact that I now had answers helped my unsteady heart find its bearings. The truth still felt like a stab to the heart.

"I mean ..." He looked up. "The last time ..." His gaze darted down at his glass. Whatever it was, the perfect eye contact he'd been maintaining all night had disappeared. "I guess what I'm trying to say is"—he rubbed his arms—"I wanted to try to forget ... you know, the day at the lake when we were all alone ..."

I didn't think he was going to bring this up.

"Hey, we don't need to talk about this, Joe. If I've upset you, I can just get the bill and go."

"No ... no." He rubbed his arms. "Why did you do it?"

"Do what?"

He could probably sense that I was playing dumb. I'm no actor, but I needed to see if he and I were on the same page.

"Kiss me."

It appeared we were.

"Because I wanted to. I don't know. It was stupid. We were kids; kids do stupid things. What else is there to say?" I took a deep breath. "Sorry, Joe, I don't want to sound upset. I guess I just never got over it. I mean, you just left. Vanished. You moved out way earlier. Did you lie to me?"

"Yes and no," he said.

"What do you mean?"

"I didn't mean to lie, Dane. I'm sorry. Yes, I was honest when I first told you about when I was moving, but my parents had told me at the last minute that we needed to move sooner because my dad was needed at the school. I was just too scared to tell you ... to see you again because I thought I'd never be able to leave you. We were stupid kids, that's all. I was scared of having to say goodbye, of having to see you sad."

"So you chose not to see me at all. That's it?"

"Hey, don't say it like that."

"I don't want to sound confrontational ... Did you know my parents and I were going up to see my grandparents for the long weekend?"

"I don't remember the specifics, but I do know I was relieved when you left."

His words cut me to my core.

"Why?"

"I don't know. I couldn't reconcile with the fact that I could ever do anything to make you hate me."

"I think you've had too much to drink," I said, letting out a faint laugh.

"Maybe." He chuckled.

"I should go. Wanna trade numbers, maybe?"

"Yeah, but before we go, I should probably get this all out now. I'm pretty hammered and happier than I've been since my book got published. Dane, I never thought I'd see you again. And look at you; you look like you're ten years younger than me. You've hardly aged! It's like you've been frozen in time. I don't think I'd ever get the chance to come clean, so please ... Dane, hear me out."

"If you're not comfortable now, you don't have to."

He looked up from his drink. "It was hard at first. I had to force myself to forget. To forget everything. I threw myself at my studies and didn't look up. Academics took over my entire life. It was like I was drowning. I tried to force the memories out by signing up for sports; the training itself was overbearing at times. My entire body would ache from all the drills, pushes, and shoves. It's so easy for people to dish out all that positive thinking crap, to say that the dopamine and serotonin from physical activity is an antidote to pain. But does anyone actually fall for any of that crap? It didn't make me feel better ... but it did distract me."

He was never this open as a kid. Then again, I never got him drunk back then. I wanted to reach out and take his hand. Ask him if he was going to be okay, ask him if he needed me to be with him tonight just like he needed me when we were kids.

"I don't know. I finished class; I went to college. I have this amazing job and amazing life that people can only dream of ... But I can't help the feeling that something is missing."

"Do you have many friends, Joe?"

He took a moment to respond and then finally let out a chuckle. "Funny, I do. But for some reason, perhaps at the very back of my mind, I felt as though I was living life and accumulating all these experiences, forcing myself to remember them to the best of my ability, just so I could tell you about them one day."

The thought startled me. I'd never been good with emotional conversations. I didn't think I'd ever actually cry in front of someone, yet my eyes stung as a lump ebbed at the back of my throat.

"I've been having panic attacks," he said.

"What?"

"I don't know, man. The stress of maintaining such a life ... It's all work and no play; I don't have time for myself. It's like I'm a puppet, a puppet to my parents, even to Cassandra."

"Have you tried talking to someone about this?"

Hard as I tried, I just didn't think I had the empathetic bandwidth to say anything to him that he hadn't already heard. I wished I could've said something to make it all better. Perhaps he'd already had enough advice and sweet nothings; perhaps just staying silent and hearing him out was all he needed.

"No, I don't want anyone to know ..."

"But ..."

"I'm sorry this is too much, I shouldn't—"

"No, no."

This time, I didn't hesitate. I reached out and took his hand. He didn't move, didn't shove my hand away, didn't get up and storm off. He just sat there, the same old Joe he always was. A scared boy thrown into a world he had no idea how to navigate, bottling everything up without complaining. Shouldering his burdens and going out of his way to not make it anyone else's problem but his. Despite all this confident posturing, he was still that same timid kid.

"Sometimes I wonder what I am doing with my life. I'm supposed to be happy, but I'm just not. Sometimes I'm scared, Dane."

Here was a man who had done everything *they* (the big *them*, all of society) had told him to do to be successful: finish school, get a job, and marry. He had it all, yet still ... You could do everything right and the sickness would still find a way to eat away at you.

All the rest of us work to get to where he is now, but when we get there, is there anything?

"Joe, I—" I scowled in exasperation with myself because I had no idea what to do or say. He was inconsolable.

"Let's talk about something happier," he said, forcing a simpering smile.

"S-sure."

"Who did you end up taking to prom?"

White hot pain built in my chest. The question reminded me of everything I didn't get to do. It pulled me back down to the life I'd lived, confronted me with the fact that things most people took for granted were not afforded to me. I didn't finish high school; ergo, didn't go to prom. I didn't get to go to a fancy college, nor did I attend all the parties that came with the experience. I didn't get to make friends with people my age. I didn't have a past, nor did I have much of a future to look forward to. I stared at my half-empty glass and murmured, "I didn't go to prom."

"What, why?"

"I didn't even finish high school."

"I apologize, I didn't mean to ... If it's too personal."

"No, it's okay. Mom and I aren't on speaking terms. My parents split up, and things just got toxic, so I left and ended up here. I didn't go to prom, but I *did* get to move to New York like I wanted to."

CHAPTER 17 SUMMER OF 2019:

Joe stood by the door, his coffee in one hand and his toothbrush in the other. It was quarter to six in the morning. I was curled on the sofa under a swath of morning sun. Cassie spent the night at her aunt's place, so Joe invited me to stay the night here. We stayed up and reminisced further. This time, he got me to open up more about my loneliness. I'd never admitted to anyone that I was lonely, but Joe had a way of making me feel safe enough to be myself. He always had.

"Are you sure you don't want a lift?"

I shook my head.

He and I had spent all night cross-referencing how we recalled our childhood. It eventually reached the point past our childhood, and I gave him a glimpse of what my life was like after he'd left. Not the full picture, of course, I couldn't bear to see him hurt.

"This is the day I ran away," I said.

"Oh, I had no idea."

I coquettishly waved my hand, signaling to him that everything was fine.

"So yeah, Mother Dearest and I were having a positively riveting conversation about her favorite topic: what a fuckup I am. The conversation ended with me telling her I wished she'd fucking die of cancer."

Joe nearly choked on his coffee.

"Jeez, Dane."

"Yeah, I know."

"Then what happened?"

"The usual. She slapped me across the face. I told her 'I am leaving now. And you will never see me again.' Then I left."

"Oh shit, Dane ..."

I shrugged.

"I mean ... so, where'd you end up going?"

"Oh, I managed to stay with an uncle."

Well, he told me to call him *uncle*. The inside of the pickup truck smelled like cigarette smoke and booze. He'd asked me where I was going, and I distinctly remember saying "nowhere, and fast." Before we'd even gotten to the motel, I'd already swallowed his first salty load. I made fifty bucks that night, enough to stay in the motel a few more nights and find my next ride. But I wasn't going to tell Joe any of that.

"Do you ever miss her?"

I scoffed.

He pulled me into a hug and held me for what felt like a fleeting eternity. Just being. No tears left my eyes.

"Dane, how did you survive?"

"I don't know."

And I still don't know the answer to that.

What I did know was that children didn't choose to be born, parents chose to have kids. Parents decided to bring someone into a world of war, depression, crippling anxiety, sickness, shitty jobs, loveless marriages, drugs, peer pressure, and loss ... Hey, kid, welcome to planet Earth!

Thanks a lot, folks.

I knew it killed him to hear this, but he was the only person there for me and I at least owed him some of the truth.

"I'm sorry, Dane. I wish I'd been there, I ... Fuck, what was wrong with me?"

"Don't worry, man."

"No, I'm serious. Why did you never tell me about any of this when we were kids?"

"I don't know. I think it only started to get really bad after you left. And you know what the kids were like in that neighborhood; I didn't have anyone."

The sun rose even higher. *It's like old times.* That was what I thought as Joe held me closer. It was a pure, beautiful morning. The sky was streaked with pink cotton candy clouds reflecting the rising sun. It had been about a week since the book signing, yet it felt longer. Every moment I wasn't with Joe, I ached to be—the days stretched on and on without any respite.

The doorbell rang. Joe jumped and wiped the tears from his eye.

"You okay?" I asked.

"Dane, for once in your life, let someone ask you that question instead." He shook his head and smiled, then got up to answer the door.

Cassie looked at me, then Joe. She was slim, with wavy blonde hair and a figure-hugging navy blue summer dress. Her feline features accentuated her modelesque figure. I saw that wordless communication course through them, an electric charge flowing from one to the other as if they were deciding what to say. And then she smiled, a small, almost secretive smile, and leaned forward against the gap of the doorway into his embrace.

"So this is *the* Dane Chandler?" Cassandra chirped.

"In the flesh," I said, getting up to greet her. "I see you've heard of me."

"Oh, I have," she said, pulling me into an embrace and planting a soft kiss on my cheek.

I don't begrudge her for snagging Joe and becoming his soon-to-be lifelong partner. I will always love him, but for his benefit and happiness, if she was who he chose, I'd be content to happily love him from afar. The three of us made breakfast, buttermilk pancakes with a side of berries and cream. Joe nursed his second mug of freshly brewed coffee. I smiled at him, and he smiled back.

CHAPTER 18: SUMMER OF 2019

"I've found a guy over here who is a high roller; he's been throwing money down like no tomorrow. I tried to get him a show with this bitch, but he isn't into chicks. I showed him a picture of you, and I think he's interested. He's into some sick shit. I'm texting you the address of your co-star. Expect to need a stiff drink afterward."

Almost mechanically, I turned on the faucet and dampened my face. I was up until five this morning entertaining a client on the Red Deb. I normally kept my hours fixed to a certain time, but denying the requests of a heavy tipper—regardless of how long he required me to last—just wasn't a winning move.

I pulled off my shirt and boxers and headed into the bedroom to find something to wear. I settled on a pair of black, ripped skinny jeans and a tattered Metallica

T-shirt. My sunken eyes stared back at me in the bathroom mirror.

Unacceptable.

A couple of dabs of concealer and powder sorted that out.

"Is my co-star hot at least?"

"Fido, if I only matched you up with guys you were into, I would've never been able to pay for this lovely apartment-slash-office that you don't need to share with anyone."

Oh, Novak. Always after the money, always looking after me. A true friend indeed.

I threw back an ibuprofen and chugged a glass of water. My lips tasted salty from the festering heat of the summer night and the scars from my recent sores. I quickly glanced at my reflection in the window opposite me, tussled my hair a bit, then raced out. The hours melted by on the subway as I rode on to my destination. I was sensitive to the scrawl of shoes scaping against the floor. The thunk of footsteps lumbering uselessly away as the train stopped to let passengers off. The windows went dark as the train entered a tunnel—as if we sank into a muck, a bleak and furious dark.

~

The window admitted no light inside the decrepit apartment. The walls were stained amber with nicotine and dusted with a black coat of visible filth. A Logitech webcam similar to mine was propped up on a tripod. The filler lights had been set up around the room. Atop them was a fluorescent light fixture chaotically sputtering like strobe. On the floor was a graveyard of flies scattered about a thick blanket of dust.

On the bed lay a man fitted in nothing but an adult diaper. He was hardly a human being—he was a fucking zombie. Affixed to his mouth was an O-gag, exposing rows of rotting gum flesh and not a single tooth. On the floor beside the bed was a watery brown spill akin to a sick baby's shit.

Next to him stood another man. His obvious muscular frame was clad with a leather gimp suit. His glazed-over eyes peeked through two holes. Hung around his waist was a belt containing all manner of sharp objects.

The man on the bed was malnourished—there wasn't a single hint of fat on his face. This was a skeleton with a thin sheet of paper draped over him. His stomach was bloated like that of a pregnant woman. Raised swaths of crust lined his hide with the texture of sun-dried leaves. Curls of infected flesh adorned the skin of his face, framed by tattered clumps of hair in assorted patches.

His cheeks were hollow with points of red and deep purple. His entire torso was ravaged by blisters and rashes so flaky they would likely give way to muscle and bone if scraped. Both his legs had been amputated.

"Are you Novak's guy?" The leather-clad man looked at me, then flitted his gaze toward the specimen shackled to the bed. "I've got your co-star right here."

A gag lurched up my throat.

"So, what do I do?"

"We're going to make a movie. This is your co-star, Eddie."

"Elaborate."

"I'm going to tell you what to do, and if you don't do it, I'll be sure to report back to Novak. If I don't give him a favorable report, he's going to make your life a living hell. Got that, kid?"

Kid.

"Gotcha."

"How old are ya, anyway?"

I just shrugged.

"We're live. All right, Fido. Get his diaper off and rim him. Be a good little bitch."

I crawled onto the bed beside Eddie and unhooked his diaper. The musky smell of human waste instantly registered as I peeled off the loose cotton. Eddie's ass was caked with feces and dried blood. He got on his hands and stumps, baring his ass to the ring light. His anus was a meaty cave of lumpy cysts protruding from light tufts of brittle hair. There was a tender red lump the size of a golf ball right by his taint that resembled a dog's tumor.

I leaned in and licked a circle around his gaping pucker. He responded to my tongue, bucking backward as his asshole clenched and dilated. My tongue flicked around the crusted beads lining the rim of his entrance. The taste was metallic and salty.

"Bite into them."

I spread Eddie's hole wide and buried my tongue into him. He grinded his ass backward, meeting the strokes of my tongue. I emerged only to take a breath. Diving back in, I chewed into a cyst and slurped at the fluid-filled sacs.

"Oh, fuck yes ... Just like that. Get the big one now," the gimp man groaned.

Looking at the camera, I pushed the blood and pus past my tongue, letting the viscid concoction dribble down my chin. I then shifted my attention to the cyst and sucked it between my teeth. I gnawed at it, breaking past the barrier of skin. The sac instantly burst, coating my tongue with an unpleasantly salty citrus blend. I slurped up the soupy excrement, extracting as much briny fluid as I could. A trickling stream of creamy matter leaked out of his rectum, forming a pool beneath him. Its stench alone was enough to nearly force the stomach acid from my constricting throat.

"Fuck, fuck! Yes, lick it clean."

The gimp man flipped Eddie onto his back. His nude body was more revolting than mine.

"Lick him. Now."

Girding my stomach, I ran my tongue across his abrasion-spattered chest. My tongue trailed around one of his stiffened nipples as I made my way to his armpits. His pit hair contained patches of white, powdery fungal gunk. Making my way down, I stroked his cock. His limp organ was a large, warty thing that jutted out of his tangled, oily pubes. Chunky, green-yellow cream seeped out of Eddie's jagged, elongated dick slit. I lapped it up, circling the head of his sick member in lazy circles.

"F-Fuck, you're good," the gimp man said.

"You like that?"

"Y-yeah, now let him fuck you."

"Got any lube?"

"No. Get creative."

And so I did.

I scraped the remaining discharge from his anal cysts into the concoction of waste in his adult diaper. I scooped up the mixture of bloody shit, sliding it down the length of his now-hard cock. He moaned as I hastened my strokes. I got into a squat position atop him and lowered myself, thrusting his dick into me. A gasp of ecstasy escaped Eddie's dry lips. I planted both my hands on his chest and thrusted myself down onto his bent prick. He bucked up his hips, thrusting into me.

My cock hardened as his member's lumpy boils brushed against my prostate. Eddie whimpered and squirmed under me, writhing in pleasure as he clenched his fists into the bed. I bent over and kissed him. The aftertaste of raw sardines registered as I brushed my tongue against his. As we moaned into each other's mouths, I bit into one of the large wart-like lumps on his lip. Foul-smelling blood coated my tongue with bitter red paste. His breath smelled of rank flatulence. We slurped at each other, transferring corrosive juices back and forth, becoming one with rot and disease.

He thrusted faster into me. His cock began to slide in and out with much more ease; I couldn't tell if it was pre-ejaculate or bloody pus from a freshly milked boil. I looked back into the viewfinder and saw that his balls and my ass were slick with viscid, dark yellow fluid. Veins in his neck tensed like centipedes travelling beneath his skin.

"Don't cum yet. The boss wants you in a full-on spit-roast."

I released a disappointed sigh and reached out for the gimp man's cock.

"You're not gonna suck me off, kid. I've got another co-star for you in the next room." He grinned, flashing a large set of rotting teeth.

The air hung heavy like a damp blanket, pulsing with a static warning.

He stepped into the bathroom and rifled around for something. Eventually, he emerged with my co-star. My body tensed as if my bones had calcified at the very prospect of what I was being asked to do. In his arms was a large Rottweiler. It was heavily sedated; its drool-soaked tongue hung limply down the side of its face like a sodden sponge. This was one of the biggest dogs I'd ever seen.

Tears webbed the corner of my eye. I sensed myself weakening. My knees buckled as if I were a single moment away from being blown over like a rootless tree amidst a hurricane. A sickening feeling coiled in my gut. Up until then, I had consented to many things—my only two limits were kids and animals. Was I actually about to break one of my rules? My heartbeat pulsed between my ears like a heron trying to break free of its cage.

"You know what to do. Trust me, you don't wanna piss Novak off."

"You seriously want me to ...?"

"Yeah, suck the dog's cock. Jerk it and blow it. Make it cum."

"Then I'm done here?"

"You're done here when I say you are."

I felt like a small island amidst a storm—acid rain pelted my feeble surface without a shred of mercy. Left with no other options, I took the dog's cock in my hand and stroked it. It didn't take much before a narrow cylinder of red muscle fully peeked out of its fuzzy shaft. It was thin and warm, requiring no more than two fingers at a time to stimulate. I tugged at it faster, willing it to prematurely cum so I could finally be done with it. I leaned over and took the animal's aroused member in my mouth. The second it met my tongue, a bitter ejaculate spilled on my taste buds and eased itself toward the back of my throat. It had the texture of an oyster with a highly concentrated saline tinge. My instincts work against my half-hearted attempt at swallowing. I instead belched a load of vomit all over the soiled sheets.

"Fuck, looks like he's about to nut!"

Eddie stilled and spasmed, ejaculating his sickness into my lower entrails. His cock secreted the horrible liquid as if a dozen oily orifices farted simultaneously. He thrusted into me a few more times as his body spasmed with post-coital aftershocks. I clenched my gut, willing the mixture of pus, semen, and blood to spurt out of me like intestinal worms.

"Very good, I knew you were as good as he said," the man said, congratulating me as if I were a trained monkey that had just performed a circus trick.

My gaze met that of the gimp man's—his eyes were wide and cautious like a hungry predator stalking defenseless prey. I stood up at a wary pace and made to slide my jeans back on.

"Not so fast."

"What do you mean?"

"We're far from done here."

"What else is there to do? I sucked the fucking dog off; this guy already came. Do you want me to make you cum?"

"Novak wants to test how committed you are to all this."

"Fine. What do I need to do?"

The gimp man reached under the bed and brought out an axe. He held it out by the handle. Was he going to make me cut off one of my limbs? Was I going to end up with stumps just like this guy on the bed?

"Novak wants you to cum in this guy's mouth."

"Okay, I'll—"

"After you decapitate him."

My heart kicked in my chest. I knew that Novak was involved in snuff films, but I didn't think he'd ever put me in one. This was something new. This was something that would keep me under his thumb forever. I already broke one of my rules with the dog, but this? Actual murder?

"I ... are you serious?"

"You're either with us or against us. Last chance, Dane."

Dane ...

"I can't."

"What?"

"Tell Novak I quit. I'm done."

"He's gonna have your head on a plate."

"I don't care if I have to be homeless again. There's no way I'm gonna kill a guy. I didn't sign up for this shit."

Before he could protest any further, I was fully dressed and past the door's threshold. I stabbed at the elevator button, slid in, and watched as the metal doors enclosed me. A reflection of death and pain glared back at me in horror from the metal doors.

The first thing I did when I got back to my apartment was beeline straight to the bathroom. I turned the water to its warmest setting and scraped off the filth of the evening's events. Nails raked into flesh as I sank to the shower floor. Strings of red and pink suds circled the white tiles on their way to the drain.

CHAPTER 19: FALL OF 2019

And then it happened again. Without warning, Joe stopped taking my calls. I'd learned a long time ago that there was no point in being upset over things one couldn't control, and I'd practiced this. But when it came to Joe, there was no way about it—I was losing my shit trying to stay calm. The days ignited forward as sulfuric thoughts seared hypervivid scenes of neglect into my psyche. The air in my apartment felt like it was charged with crackling bursts of electricity.

The nights were dark and endless.

Sleep hardly came. I spent most nights staring out the window, cigarette in hand. Ropes of dust and nicotine swayed in the fluorescent heat of the sickly yellow neon city lights as I smoked by the window. The air was opaque with the smoke of burning trash. A fuzz of city traffic echoed through the air vent in the ceiling.

Every morning passed by uneventfully, yet still, I remained anxious as ever. When I got back from one of my runs, I discovered that someone had slipped something under my door. A manila envelope. *Who did this? How did they know where I lived?*

I must've blacked out for a couple of minutes because I suddenly found myself sitting on the closed lid of my toilet and sliding my fingers under the flap of the envelope. There was no note ... only a printed glossy picture the size of a bond paper. The bottom of the envelope was stained with a dark patch. Its contents trickled out.

Inside was a picture of Joe at a restaurant with Cassandra. I instantly knew who was responsible for this.

Novak.

There Joe was, fresh-faced, having drinks after a long day at the office, wearing that light blue tie I bought him. I doubted the photographer meant to catch this, but he had managed to catch Joe's smile, his perfectly beautiful smile. The detached, artless way in which this photo had been taken sent a prickle of gooseflesh down my arms. I flipped it around and saw something written. It was a time and a link. It said I needed to access the dark web to open it.

I switched on the computer and fired up the TOR browser, then input the encrypted code.

Something popped up:

The domain you are about to enter will delete itself one minute after you enter it. This domain is protected. Its contents cannot be captured. The local host will be notified when you click enter, so expect further communication within the next few days. Do you wish to enter? Yes and No.

I hesitantly clicked Yes.

I scrolled down to a photo of a man. On the top left of the photo was a readout. This was taken from a Polaroid and then someone took a picture of the Polaroid—presumably in a different location so as not to have it traced anywhere. Whoever took this truly left no fingerprints. The timestamp indicated it was taken a week ago today—around the same night he'd stopped responding to me. Cassandra didn't know where I lived, nor did she have my contact number. She couldn't have possibly told me if he had gone missing after all this time.

I scrolled lower and saw the same photo but from different angles.

I then paused on a series of photos and screamed.

A closeup of eyes contorted in fear. A man in a leather gimp mask. A hand with a missing finger. The man was hooked up to this metal S&M contraption wrenching his mouth open. And the blood.

So.

Much.

Blood.

My hands began to shake. My breathing became more rapid as my heart kicked in my chest. I almost fell backward. I knew that Novak was vindictive. I knew that he would likely go after me since my sudden departure, but this? Why did it have to come to this? Two things breached my mind in that instant: Joe was in the clutches of very bad people, and this was all because of me. Joe wouldn't go off with just anyone, so this must've been someone he trusted. A cab driver? His friend?

I quickly hit Command + Shift + 3. The screenshot came out all black.

I pressed it again. And again. And again.

BLACK.

BLACK.

BLACK.

BLACK.

BLACK.

A sharp cramp seized my gut. I kicked my rucksack open and took out my phone to take pictures of all of it. The second I got into my camera app, the entire screen had gone black. The envelope was still heavy, I desperately shook it to dislodge the rest of its contents.

Out fell a finger.

A finger with a snake tattoo coiled around it.

My phone rang.

It was an unknown number. I swiped the answer bar and held the device to my head. I waited for someone to say something, anything. The longer the silence drew on, the harder my heart jabbed into my ribcage.

"Bet you thought you could just escape from him, now, didn't you? Dane, you're his pet. You'll always be his fucking pet."

"W-who ... who are you? What have you done to him?"

But there was no point in me asking what'd been done to him, now, was there? His mouth was hooked up to a metal O-gag. Several teeth had been wrenched loose, others cracked. Pink foam dribbled down his chapped lips. His neck and chest were littered with bruises and burn welts. His left eye was blood-shot and bruised; his nose, completely splintered. He was strapped to the inside of a metal tub with barbed wire clinging to his torso. A knife was held to his neck.

"He's not going to get away with this. He's not going to."

"The way I see it, you're in no position to make threats. You call the cops? He dies."

"What do you want?"

No response.

And so I sat there, pathetically, not knowing what to say or do. If I didn't cooperate, then what? Would they send Joe back to Cassie in pieces? Would he be found dead in a ditch somewhere? The guy who looked back at me in the mirror looked ten years older than normal; he looked as old as he was. Dark patches lined the corners of my eyes, my face was pale, and my lips were chapped raw from all the nervous, unconscious biting. Then—

"Are you still on the line?"

"Y-yes."

"You are going to do exactly as I say. If you don't listen to me, there will be consequences. Got that?"

"Yes."

"If you agree to play, say: I'm a piece of shit faggot."

"Fuck you!"

"Your boyfriend is losing a lot of blood, by the way."

A scream on the other end of the line made my blood freeze. It was raspy and labored, like someone who hadn't been given a drink of water in days.

"No! Stop!"

"Say it, bitch."

I frowned; tears welled up in my eyes as I whispered, "I'm a piece of shit faggot."

"Come on, you can do better than that."

"I'm a piece of shit faggot, all right!?"

"Well done."

"What have you done with him?"

"Nothing that'll kill him. But we're just getting started. Would you like to keep playing for his life?"

"Yes."

Because what else was there to do?

"To keep playing, say: My useless faggot self drinks dog piss."

I gritted my teeth. "My useless faggot self drinks dog piss."

"Great. So here's what's going to happen. I'll tell you to do something. If you complete the task, this guy lives. If you fuck it up, I'll make sure he loses more blood. Rest assured, I'll be very creative. Also, we've hacked into your desktop. Do the tasks in front of the webcam. You've got an audience."

"Look, what do you want me to do, man?"

"First of all, you can call me Sir."

"Sorry, Sir."

"Good. Now we can begin. Get in front of your desktop."

And so I did. I sat in front of my desktop, willing divine intervention of any sort to happen, willing Joe to stay alive long enough for me to help him.

"I want you to pull out one of your nails."

"What? H-how?"

"Figure it out. Or he's fucking dead."

I pulled the drawer open and saw it: a box cutter. Taking a deep breath, I paused as I pushed the sharp blade up. It was still stained with flecks of dried blood from my last cutting session. I balled up the collar of a used kitchen towel and stuffed it in my mouth, biting down. I then held the tip of the blade under my nailbed and pushed. The pain came instantly—so strong and sharp I could feel it traveling down my arms and up my neck. I yipped out a helpless cry as I dug the metal in further.

"Yes, cry for me, you little shit. Give me something to jerk it to."

I grinded my teeth into the damp cloth and pushed the metal into the crease beneath the nail. It made a wet, cracking noise as it slid into the resistant flesh of the nailbed. The nail bent backward like hard plastic as it parted from the skin. The further back I pried, the louder my unholy screams came. Blood seeped out of the ruptured nailbed as I wriggled it free from the connective lining of dry skin.

And then it was loose.

I was left with nothing more than a patch of hypersensitive nerves and shredded skin.

I threw the boxcutter to the floor and pinch my eyes shut, crying into the kitchen towel. I held the back of my hand up to the camera to prove my compliance.

"F-fuck ..." I groaned.

"Good. Now, if you want to keep playing, say: I like to suck my daddy's cock."

I watched the world blink in and out of existence, flaring like the last frames of an old film stock spinning loose from its reel. I sucked in and tightened my core, willing myself to bear the pain.

"I ... I like to suck my daddy's cock."

"Good. Now, make yourself shit on the floor."

This wasn't the first time one of Novak's clients had made such a request. I knew exactly what to do. I took out an enema bulb and water-based lube from my black box and held it up to the light. I rushed to the sink and filled the bulb of the enema with lukewarm water, then lubricated the tip of the nozzle before pulling down my pants. I squatted over the nozzle, easing it into me. With the lubed tip inside, I squeeze about a quarter of the water in, then fell to my knees. A minute passed before I felt the sensation I knew all too well.

"I know you were a fucking fudge-packer for your actual daddy. Novak showed me some of those hurtcore tapes. I love jerking it to them every now and then."

I said nothing in response. The weight of the sloshing liquid grew heavy as I pushed. Clumps of shit eased past the musculature of my sphincter and fell to the floor in successive splats.

"Eat it, bitch. And don't you dare spit anything out."

Without protest, I reached down and picked up the raw scat. I raised a clump to my mouth and instantly shuddered. The mound of shit was as bitter as one thousand proof of alcohol; the texture was fibrous yet oily like avocado. I mashed the salty scat on my tongue before shoveling more shit into my maw. The aftertaste was a pastiche of concentrated salty bile. As I made to force it down my throat, fecal fluids squeezed past the gaps of my teeth with fresh saliva like black coffee grounds. Once I swallowed everything, I sucked my fingers, cleaning them of the raw, acidic juices.

"I hope you liked that, Sir," I said, smiling with brown teeth.

"Very good."

"What's next?" I sighed, resigned to my dark fate.

"Meet me outside in five. Don't bring anything."

The phone line went dead.

I kicked the chair and ran to the bathroom. Hot puke belched out of me before I could reach the rim of the toilet. I pulled my sweater sleeve over my wrist and wiped my congested nose. I then jammed my shoes onto my feet and swung the door open. The entrance of my building led to a series of empty alleyways. My vision was clouded by scalding tears. A million thoughts raced through my head at lightning speed.

Joe is in danger. This is all my fault. This can't be happening. There's no way I am awake now. I'll wake up any second. Why was there so much red? Why was there so much red in his hair? Is my Joe still alive?

My restless train of thought was interrupted when heavy footsteps ran close behind me. I turned, but it was too late. A massive hand clamped over my eyes and mouth. I kicked out, fighting off my assailant. As I managed to slide out of his grip, his fist connected with my nose. Before I knew it, I was back in his clutches again with a damp cloth affixed to my lips and nose. I'd broken Novak's rules, and this was my punishment. I squirmed around anxiously, but it was of no use. My vision dimmed as if I'd just driven into a black tunnel without my headlights.

And then everything went black.

CHAPTER 20: NOW

The Puppetmaster unchains Joe and lifts him out of the tub. Maybe they don't expect him to move anymore; maybe they know he has no chances left due to his worn state. Or maybe they're going to—

"No!" I yell.

The thought that I could lose him becomes more and more real with each passing second. The fact that I've managed to survive this long is hopefully a good sign. I need to keep fighting.

Sadie smiles at me with her yellow teeth, and I shudder in revulsion.

"Uncuff him."

What?

She leans in front of me with a key and slips it into the shackles binding my arms.

"Don't worry, I know you're not going to try anything stupid. If you do, he gets it. Understand?"

I nod.

Joe's gaze is downcast. He is propped up on his knees and being held up only by his hair. If there's any pain in this, none of it registers on his face. His features wear the expression of a hollow husk—utterly empty and spent. Gelatinous pink drool oozes out of his mouth like maple syrup. His eyes are so bruised and gummy it's impossible to tell if he's even got them open. His lower lip droops down, giving me a glimpse of a row of shattered teeth.

"What's the next task?"

The masked man regards me. "Look at you; I am appreciating this enthusiasm. You've been putting on a great show for everyone at home."

"Just tell me what I have to fucking do!"

"Very well."

He tosses a rusty meat cleaver at my feet. "You have five minutes to pick which hand you like more and chop the other one off."

My bowels turn to water.

"W-what ...?"

"I'm starting the timer now. One."

"No, wait, I don't know what to do—"

"Two."

"You want me to—Are you fucking insane!?"

"Hmmm ... Seven."

"No! Fuck!"

I don't know if I can do it, but I have to try. My gag reflex shudders as I reach for the handle of the cleaver. I lie on my side, hold out my left hand, and raise the blade above it. And then I swing. The metal cuts into my wrist with a *thwack*. I begin sawing into the flesh just below my palm. Blistering pain blasts through my body as the sound of shredding meat tears through the room. Wet tendons crack and bones crunch.

I hoist the blade back up and throw it down again. As it jams further into my flesh, blood spurts out of the gummy muscle. Squirting blood drenches my upper arm, my neck, and torso. My arm stops as the blade jams into the bone. I grit my teeth tighter and push further in, tugging the cleaver back and forth like it's a saw. A squishy, crackling sound emerges as I push and pull on the handle.

The exercise requires more effort as I wrench the blade up and hack away at meddlesome bone and muscle. The blade again jams, forcing me to violently yank it back and bring it down. Squelching and crunching sounds bounce off the walls in tandem with my screams. Blood squirts and floods out from severed arteries as I finally make it to the layer of flesh and muscle beneath the bone.

And then it's over.

"Th-there ..." I rasp.

"Yippeee, Daddy! I wanna!"

"What would you like to do, my dear?"

"Stump fuck! Stump fuck!"

"Okay, pet. But first we must make sure our little plaything doesn't bleed out."

And that's when, in my delirious state, I see a yellow glow grow in my foggy vision. Heat builds as it nears me, and then searing pain from the fires of hell itself shoots up my left arm. My hand lies on the floor, yet I feel like it's still attached to me and someone has dipped it into molten lava.

"Yes, Sadie, just like that!"

Metal clangs on the floor. The tip is still orange—a branding iron used for cattle.

"Okay. You've had your fun. Now, please ... just let him go ..." I rasp.

"Oh, Fido. I hope you're not going to miss your little friend here. It's disposal day," Sir says, as he picks up Joe's limp hand to make him act like he's bidding me goodbye.

"Say bye-bye," Sadie says, holding up his chin to make him look at me.

"Don't touch him, you sick fuck! Put him down now or else I'll fuck you up! I swear, I'll—"

"I don't know why you're so pissed." Sadie cuts me off. "This guy's been dead for weeks. He was dead even before you got here."

What?

No, this can't be. I stop and stare, unable to process what I just heard. If I move a muscle, I feel like my skin will crack like cellophane. Her words hit me like an electroconvulsive shock-induced jolt. This whole time ... this whole time ... Joe ... There was nothing I could've done. Nothing I could've done to save ...

Sadie hands Puppetmaster the bloody cleaver. The weapon casts a distinct shadow on the ground. And then there's the sound of the blade. Metal on air—that distinct *whoosh* of the swing comes down to a *thunk*. Then come the tearing sounds, then the gurgle, then the pop and crackle of joints being dislodged. He swings the axe down again and again, each blow rattling the wooden ceiling above us. The thick blade slips right through Joe's blue-green flesh, jamming at the bone.

My feet go numb. My remaining hand locks in a crow's fist. A scream that comes from a place beyond fury, a banshee howl from hell, rips out of me.

"Yes, Daddy, yes!" Sadie chirps.

Sadie sits next to Joe, masturbating with the handle of a rusty knife. She screams in pleasure as he swings the axe down again, right on the joint above Joe's humerus, unlinking his arm from his shoulder. He brings the axe up and then flings it down again, hacking at his clavicle. Joe's tough exterior is his last and final form of protest. I wring my eyes shut as the burning sensation is exacerbated by my labored panting.

"And now it's time for baby's first stump fuck. Just like what I promised!"

Before I can move, the Puppetmaster is behind me. He wrenches my jaw open and forces a pill into my mouth. I try to spit it out, but he clamps his hand over my mouth and nose. And so I swallow. The effect is almost instantaneous. A tingle drops to the base of my spine as my cock stiffens.

"Now, it's time for the climax. You're going to fuck your dead friend like I know you've always wanted to."

He shoves me forward. The shackles binding my ankles pull them out from under me, causing me to fall to my side. He kicks me onto my back. Tears burn in my eyes as I sob.

"I'm sorry, Joe. I'm so ... s-sorry."

Sadie spits on her hand and strokes my cock. Sir stomps on my right arm, holding it in place. I squeeze my eyes shut, willing the world out of existence. And then I feel the cold softness enveloping my cock. Joe's stiff ass. I open my eyes and see Joe's dead face looking down at me. Sir's hands hold him up by the shoulders as Sadie adjusts his hips over mine. She shoves him down on my involuntary erection, then shifts onto her back. Legs spread, she takes my bleeding stump and eases it into her diseased cunt.

"Yes, baby! Fuck that bloody stump!"

"Fuck, Daddy, it's so nice and warm! Better than any dick I've had!"

Sadie pumps my amputation in and out of her and moans. Sir thrusts Joe's corpse onto me, making me rape him against my will. The entire world blurs as bright lights above us illuminate this grotesque spectacle. Across from me is a camera live-streaming this footage to who knows how many people.

And then Joe is off me.

When I dare look up, the Puppetmaster holds Joe's severed arm up to his mouth like a chicken leg. He raises his mask and sinks his teeth into Joe's rotting flesh. He bites a chunk of the arm, tearing into the flesh like a rabid dog, shaking his head back and forth. He bites down further and squeezes the thickened black sludge out of it like a grimy sponge. He gets on all-fours and plants a deep kiss on Sadie's mouth. Their bloody tongues slither against one another, staining their teeth deep crimson as bubbling blood and saliva trickle down onto Sadie's breasts. Blood rushes to my head. My fury would be enough to scorch this entire fucking planet.

"For someone with the innocent face of an angel, you have a dead look in your eyes that would frighten a seasoned terrorist. Heck, I think I get a bit of goosebumps just looking at you."

I want to tear his eyes out and feed them to him and then drown him in boiling oil.

"Oops, chopping up your friend over here seems to have resulted in a little accident." He looks down.

I meet the direction of his gaze and realize that this supposed accident is his erection. He's fucking hard. He then unzips his pants and frees his veiny, crooked prick. He wets his hand with some of Joe's blood and strokes himself.

"Fuck, that's better ..."

The sight of him makes Sadie fuck herself with my amputation even harder. She shoves the hilt of my bone deeper and rubs her clit with her other hand. Her wet, wart-infested cunt makes squelching noises as she penetrates herself. Boils dot the ridges of her beefy sex like pore-sized lumps teeming with parasites. Blisters pop against bloody flesh as she rides toward her orgasm.

"I wonder how stiff this guy's asshole is," he says.

"I'm going to fucking kill you," I say through gritted teeth.

"I'd tell you to shut your fuck-slut mouth, but frankly, the sound of you getting angry is making me harder."

He cracks his knuckles and his neck and looks down at Joe.

No ... no.

"Hey, kitty, did you come yet?" he asks.

"No, Daddy, not yet."

He lifts Joe by the head. Joe's jaw is completely limp. His tongue hangs out of his mouth like a wilted petal; one eye is rolled to the back of his head, and the other one is completely bruised and bloodshot. His lips are black, his cheeks have been torn off, and his nose is a gore-caked, flattened stump. He has a head, a torso, and bone stumps where his extremities once were.

Sir then drags the body up to me and holds the axe to my neck, pressing it so tight that a burning sensation sears beneath the layer of muscle and nerves. A line of blood streams down my chest and down to the floor.

"Don't look away. The fun isn't anywhere near over."

He holds Joe's head to his erection and plunges his cock into the corpse's throat, fucking the head of my favorite person. Tendons snap; bones crack. The smacking sound of his repeated thrusts vibrates off the walls. He shoves his cock in so far that Joe's throat bulges. He then pulls out and positions himself in front of Sadie, aggressively frigging himself with rotting corpse fluid. The frenzied rubbing noise is met with a savage grunt. Fresh spunk jets out of his cock and all over Sadie's face. She laps it up, and globs of it slip out of the gaps of her missing teeth. He then puts his hand on her throat and shoves his cock into her maw again. She gags and spasms as he throat-punches her into next week.

"Get ready for the volcano!"

He pulls his cock out and an explosion of puke shoots out about three feet in front of her. He then picks up a handful of puke and smothers the putrid, chunky liquid all over my face.

I don't flinch; I don't react. There is no panic. There is no fear. I've just given up; all my will to live has dissipated. All my love was in Joe, and now Joe is gone.

He shoves Joe into a disposable plastic bag—a container of entrails that will serve as his final resting place.

"Here's a souvenir for ya, kid. Enjoy it while you last."

He tosses Joe's half-eaten arm at me. I do nothing ... feel nothing. He slams the door behind him. I shrink into myself and fall into a black, dreamless abyss. The last thing I hear are his loud, thudding footsteps ascending the stairs, heading into the world, undetected. Something untangles inside me, something that shouldn't have loosened. A stitch has come undone.

CHAPTER 21: NOW

I've been left in the dark for who knows how long. I think I've managed to drift into sleep several times, but I can't vouch for its quality. I don't know how much blood I lost. My one arm is cuffed to the corner of the tub, while my other has been wrapped up in duct tape.

My heightened senses tell me the Puppetmaster is back upstairs. Sadie's vile, gravelly voice says that he should've let me bleed out because she wants "new toys to play with." He responds by saying that viewers like me and want to see my death play out at a leisurely pace.

A piercing white beam of light shines as the door kicks open. Sadie's scrawny, crack-bitch legs come into blurred focus. She scowls in frustration as she shoves a piece of bread against my chapped lips. It's stale and musky. I resist at first, until she rubs the hard bread on my bruised and bloodied lips, which she eventually parts. A tinge of mold and mildew instantly registers. It takes everything in me to stifle back the gag.

"That's more than any of the others got, you little shit. I ain't no waitress, and this ain't no fucking restaurant. I wanted you to be dead anyway," she says, forcing another few pieces of bread into my mouth. Frustrated with my inability to swallow, she punches me square on the kisser. My head snaps back, then hangs forward, chin to chest.

She heads back upstairs.

If I could, I'd resist the food and die of hunger. I know Joe wouldn't want any more death. He wouldn't want ...

Fuck that. He's dead. And so am I.

I yank and pull and push and shove at the metal claws digging into my wrist. My skin tears as gouts of fresh, warm blood flow. Hand lubricated with gore, I force my wrist through the cuff. I grind my teeth so hard my jaw aches, and I pull and I wrench until a flap of skin hangs like a latex prop and blood spouts into the humid air. With a firm bite and a sharp exhale, my hand is free.

At last, I roll out of the tub and lie on the cold, dank floor. Too much time on the cold ground turns the entire left side of my body numb, which eventually turns into pins and needles.

Footsteps thunder above me again. Looks like Sadie isn't finished with me.

Three ...

Two ...

One ...

The rusty door squeaks on its hinges. The stench of Sadie's breath, the sound of her breathing ... She's coming closer. As she leans in toward me, I flex my knee and kick with all my might. My foot connects. The blow is subsequently met with a *clang* and *thud*.

"Y-you ... fuck ..." She groans, gasping for air.

A distinct *whoosh* of a blade cutting through the air instantly registers as she swings her hand around. He must've sent her down with a weapon in case something like this was to happen. With reckless abandon and nothing to lose, I lunge at her. Eyes closed, my shoulder connects.

A metal *clink*.

She's dropped her weapon.

Greasy finger-like talons cinch themselves into my bicep. The pain screams through my nerves in intermittent surges as I shove her face down and slam the back of her head into the concrete. Her skull collides with the cement like a cracking egg.

Her body stills, but her chest still ebbs with life.

Through an opaque haze, I manage to locate her weapon: a small, serrated kitchen knife. I pick it up and cut my feet loose.

As my vision sharpens, I am met with her alarmed gaze. It's as if her ego and misconception about having the upper hand has been challenged for the very first time. I grab her by her ratty hair and raise my knee at her gut. She shrinks backward. The way she looks at me tells me one thing: this dumb bitch realizes she's fucked.

"Please ... let me go. I-I'll suck your cock!" She nods, smiling.

"Do you enjoy this?" I say.

She begins to sob. Her chest heaves up and down as snot bubbles pop from her nose. She hysterically screams and flails about as if she has a chance.

"No. No! I swear. He said he'd kill me if I didn't. It's his fault. I didn't do nothing!"

"You ate parts of me. You masturbated as he fucked Joe's corpse."

"Fuck you! I'll do anything. I'll let you fuck me. You can shove it in my ass. That's what you queers like, right? Right? I'll suck your cock; just please don't kill me!" she wails hysterically.

Black lines of mascara run down her sand-dry skin.

"Actually, I'd rather put my dick in a wood chipper ..."

Before she can respond, I kick her in the gut so hard she falls to her side. A rank puddle of urine and blood pools between her legs. The stench of it reminds me of when she pissed on my face.

"Please ..." she mumbles.

"Please, what? What?!"

"I'm pregnant," she rasps.

I laugh. I laugh so loud I can see her visibly wince.

"Yeah?"

"Yeah! I'm going to ... to run away and be a good mama to ... my—"

"You're both gonna die tonight, and your baby will be raped in hell." I stomp on her face so hard cartilage splinters under my heel. "And so are you." My heel twists into her face with all my strength. "Bitch!"

I take the knife and stab her so hard in the cheek that the blade grits against teeth. I drag the blade along her gore-soaked flesh and down to her two rows of yellow incisors. Hot, red sap spreads all over my knuckles. I drive the blade in deeper, stabbing the inside of her mouth. The gurgling sound reminds me of boiling oil.

"Not much to say now, huh, fucking dirty bitch?"

I yank the knife out and spit on her face. And then I jab the tip of the knife into her eye. Her eye socket spits out a wet *pop* as it yields and sucks at the blade as I withdraw it. Thick orbital fluids spout out like a boiled egg being squeezed of its yolk.

Still, she fights back, bucking uselessly at me, unable to scream because of all the blood accumulating in her mouth.

I scan the room and reach for the table for a couple of the doctor's instruments. The first thing I set my sights on is the pliers. I stand on top of Sadie and kick her head so hard that her jaw cracks out of place.

"Hnnnhgg!! Hnnghh!" is all she says in protest.

I take the pliers and hook them onto her bottom two lower central incisors. Clamping down, I twist and tear as her yellow gnashers give way to the cold, gritty steel. It doesn't take much, considering the level of decay they were in, but I manage to jimmy a couple of them free of the gums. The beet-red roots cling onto her pus-dried gums as I then mangle her tusk free from its muscled hood. I then work on her top central incisors, cracking them down the center to make my job easier. They give, splintering like the brittle plaster of a dilapidated building. Her maw fills with black blood that has the consistency of spoiled gelatin.

Her jaw hangs limp as her tongue dangles limply like a newly defrosted cold cut. I take the pruning shears and clip them onto the tip of her tongue.

"Here's some advice, hun. Men don't like it when you open your bitch mouth to do anything other than suck a cock."

I clamp the shears onto the wet slab of her tongue, clipping through it like I'm cutting into a fatless chicken breast.

"You like that, huh? Bitch! I'm nowhere near done with you."

Her one working eye is wide like she can't believe what is happening. I take a serrated knife and plunge it into the stump that remains of her nose. As I saw into the smashed cartilage, the blade jams into bone. I press the hilt of the knife down like a lever and pulley my way through the outer tissue. It cracks free like a walnut, leaving only skin to worry about. Pulling the rubbery texture back, I leave her with a black crater in the center of her face.

A musky smell invades my nose—I look down and am reminded of the puddle of piss.

"No, no, we can't have that now, can we?"

She shakes her head.

"Here, let me clean you up."

I pick up a bottle and unscrew the lid. The pungent aroma instantly bleaches my senses. I tip the container over and pour the acid right onto her cunt. The folds of her labia pop and sizzle; her layers of flesh pull back like shy children, exposing the membranous layer of muscle beneath. Her eye stays open, desperate and erratic.

"I hope that hurt," I say, hocking a loogie at her mangled face.

I pick up my next instrument of torture: the doctor's belt sander. I rev the device to life and dangle it in front of her face. She squirms and cries as I tease her. I then lower the device. The coarse sandpaper begins disintegrating the loose flesh of her right breast. Her thin top instantly tears off, revealing her flat, hollowed-out tit. The coarse sandpaper skids alongside her flesh, scraping it down to the meat. Bloody chunks splat all over like cherries being blended without a lid. The dismantled raw meat that was once her breast splits open; yellow, fatty clumps fly up at me and the wall behind her. I push the device so hard that the white of her bones peeks through the torn, raw flesh. Even if she could scream, it would be drowned out by the loud drilling sound.

Picking up a Taser, I press it against her left breast and squeeze. Her entire body shakes in convulsions as I press the prongs deeper and deeper into her burning flesh. Her one eye is wide open and glazed over; her hollowed-out lips shudder from the current zapping through her body.

I then take the rusting shears to her chemically burned labia. Prying open her diseased flap, I clamp the blades down, splitting the wet muscle down the middle. It oozes viscous clots of blood down the center. The blood that gushes out is watery and thin, soaking both my feet.

Her sturdy body begins to slacken as a wave of blood pools beneath me. I then shear past the flesh of her pubis and up to her belly button. I twist the blades, widening the hole as her tough flesh satisfyingly gives way. Cold metal cuts into warm flesh, biting into the membrane and connective tissue.

Locking my gaze to her one eye, I bury my fingers into the hole, digging my fingers into the warm silk of her innards.

"Hu-ahh-auhhh ..." she rasps.

I look right into her eye as I fist the cave to her exposed entrails, digging through the fleshy wet tubes. Clenching a fistful of guts, I yank my hand out of her cavernous incision. Her unspooled guts scatter to the floor alongside a pulpy stew of gelatinous fluids and feces.

I drape the slippery tubes over her and then cut into them with the shears. Gaseous air, intestinal sewage, and clumps of thick blood sluice out of the incision like earthworms.

Pressure builds in my crotch. Looking down, I see that I am hard. I am a sick fuck, aren't I? I pull out mangled tubes from her body and slide them against the leaking tip of my aroused member. I bend over her, thrusting my cock into the cavernous maw of unspooled intestines, bucking forward and back.

Fuck, this is better than the tightest asshole I've fucked. Nothing compares to this—nothing. All she can do is look up at me in a state of shock as I rape the inner workings of her sick body. I plunge my infected cock deeper and deeper into her. Pus sacs from my pubis burst with the force of my thrusts as I still and shiver into orgasm. Yellow, pulpy jizzum spurts from my cock, all over her unraveled digestive tract.

I stand and give her one last kick to the head before I bury the blade so deep into her neck it scrapes against the floor. I rip the knife out, pocket it, and make my way up the stairs.

~

Squeezing my eyes shut and gritting my teeth, I push back as far as my weakened legs will allow. Leaving the door to the basement slightly ajar, I shift forward and head into the room. Scooching my bum on the floor, I thrust forward and back to gain traction. I then slam into something—the leg of a table, most likely. Pain screams from the small of my back as I roll to my side.

I reach up and, sure enough, find the table's corner. I force out a sharp exhale, clench my jaw, and haul myself up.

I walk slowly, rolling my feet from heel to toe, willing the silence to mask my presence. Every few steps, I stop and listen. The front door is secured by large chain.

The house is very quiet, save for the odd patter of drizzle on the windowpane signaling an oncoming shower. The only other thing I can hear is my breathing and the loud thud of my heart. The house seems awfully dark. I couldn't recall being in a dark space this long, since I was used to the bright lights of the filming equipment downstairs.

I shut my eyes and open them. It makes no difference; my vision refuses to adjust.

Blackness.

The moment I straighten my back, a dam of pain bursts, assaulting my back, legs, anus, neck, head ... Everything hurts, but the worst pain is in my chest, knowing that Joe has left the world a darker place than it was just a couple of weeks before. Before today, I thought I knew what pain was. I didn't know shit.

Joe. Joe is in the basement. He is now nothing more than a corpse among corpses. I will never see him again *Joe.*

I pause to take inventory of myself. I sidestep to the left until my arm brushes softly against the tattered wallpaper. I can't shake the feeling that I am being watched. That the walls are somehow closing in on me.

The door to the basement is about ten feet away from me on my right. My best bet is a phone. I can't move. My body is telling me to move, but my mind tells me that if I so much as breathe too loudly or move a muscle, I will alert him to my presence.

I lean on the wall for more support as my eyes begin to adjust to the darkness. Unwilling to test fate, I double back through the threshold of an open set of doors and find a stairway. Baby steps: one, two, one, two.

And then I see a sliver of light.

From a door.

A door that swings open.

"Fuck ..." I whisper.

And then I see that the door upstairs is swinging back and forth as if being manipulated by a faint draft from the second floor.

Maybe he left one of the windows open?

I inch myself forward, hand brushing against the cruddy wall, until I bump into a jutting edge of wood.

A banister.

Ascending the stairs, I clutch the handrail for dear life, tasting nothing but bitter copper and salt, leaning forward so I don't fall back down the stairs and break something and ruin all my hard work. If I've already made it this far, this must mean something.

With each step, a different part of my body cramps up. I resort to just closing my eyes and not looking up. Feel, don't see. Do, don't think. Eventually, a large, flat swath of wood meets the tip of my foot. I've made it to the landing.

Maybe he left it open. Maybe he's in there right now.

Maybe Sadie used the bathroom before she came down to me? I didn't see any other bathrooms inside the house.

That's gotta be it.

Something clangs in the distance.

I suck in a quick breath.

I clutch Sadie's knife in my right hand and hold it ahead of me. I stop the door by placing my hand on the doorknob. Fluorescent lights glow overhead. The hallway is lit with a pale yellowish amber from the room. I look down and notice that I've left a trail of blood behind me and on the doorknob.

Brilliant.

I turn it, failing the first few times because of my blood-slicked fingers. The knob eventually gives, and I push through.

A bathroom.

I practically fall to my knees, barrelling straight toward the sink. I pull the faucet toward me and let a torrent of cold water gush freely. I bend down despite the pain and rub all the viscera from my face and hair. I reach for a washcloth and scrape all the residue from my face. I then cup my hand under the cascading stream and bring the water to my lips. It isn't enough. I bend lower, craning my neck at an odd angle, unleashing pain so great it feels like a metal rod has been surgically inserted into the top of my spine. I push past the pain and suck in the cold, nourishing water. I choke and retch into the sink, coughing hard ... only to twist my head back upward again to desperately slurp in the cool, revitalizing liquid.

I stand up and see myself in the mirror for the first time in days. I look like I've aged ten years. Gone is my youthful glow. Gone is the shine in my eyes. I look emaciated, my cheekbones are more prominent, and the blood vessels in my left eye are so red from the multiple beatings I'd taken.

I carefully shuffle out of the bathroom and push past the next door. Furniture is sparse, and there isn't much to indicate that either of them lives here. There's one neatly made bed and nothing else to hint at who either of these people is outside of these walls. Only enough light filters in to let me see vague, blurred shapes. I hold my breath, anticipating movement.

Nothing.

No one is lying on the bed.

What if he's in the room with me, hiding?

What if he's under the bed?

No, there's no way he can be here. I can hear everything; surely his breathing or something would have alerted me to his presence.

Find out. Turn on the lights.

But if I turn my back to the bedroom, this could give him enough time to jump out and pounce me.

A chill worms its way through my insides. For a second there, I think I hear the slow groan of snoring.

Just then, a crack of lighting jolts me out of my senses. It puts me on high alert. But it also, for a fraction of a second, lights up the entire room like a camera flash. I am in here alone.

Phew.

Across the room is a cabinet.

I slowly pull the door open and find a set of dirty blood-stained clothes. These were likely where he stashed the belongings of some of his prior victims like some sick kind of memento. I pull a black shirt over my head and slip into a pair of cargo shorts.

I lock the door behind me and flick the light switch on. As the brightness stings my eyes, I half-expect to see a masked demon leap out at me with a butcher axe.

Nothing but empty stillness.

The first thing I look for is a landline. *Who has landlines these days?* I slip the knife into my waistband and jerk open the top drawer of the nightstand. A leather binder. A photo album of sorts. I crack it open and instantly want to vomit. Inside the photo album is a collection of Polaroids. Admittedly, he did have an eye for composition and lighting.

One photo is of a woman; her chest and stomach have been sawed open. Her flesh was inelegantly torn off, leaving the inside of her body on full display. All her organs have been excavated and lie beside her. Another is of a woman whose breasts have been sliced off and whose teeth had been reduced to cracked splinters. Her legs are nailed far apart, and a fire burns under her, roasting her vagina. Several other photos are lingering on her screaming face, others are of her burning crotch.

The most horrific one is of a young boy; his face has been completely caved in by a blunt object, and his legs, arms, and genitals have been chopped off and set down in a circle around him. His abdomen has been cut open, exposing his meat and bone. On the following page is that same boy bent over the tub being raped by a German Shepherd.

In another series of images is a young girl. Bite marks riddle her underdeveloped breasts and shoulders. Hand-print-shaped bruises wrap around her arms and neck. A half-shattered bottle has been rammed into her hairless vagina, her entire groin area ravaged with contusions and lacerations. Another photo is her bent over; bleeding fissures line her dilated anus. The name *Tully* is scrawled at the bottom of this particular photo. I close the album shut and set it down on the bed.

I whirl around and make my way out of the room and back into the hallway. Nothing. Darkness. Everything looks still. No light comes from the slats beneath the doors of any of the rooms.

I lurch down the hall, moving as silently as possible. Ball, heel, ball, heel … The air in the hallway is so thin it feels like a transient draft moving against my skin.

I make my way back downstairs to the kitchen. I pull the refrigerator door open and see some beers and a loaf of bread. Can't do the beer—gotta keep a clear head. I grab the loaf of bread. By the sink is a stack of used dishes. I fill up a glass with water from the tap, then take a bite out of the slice of bread. My stomach protests because it's grown unused to food—on top of that, this bread is moldy. I chew and swallow in small bites, forcing the bread down.

Breathe. Chew. Swallow. Sip.

I look up, breathe, swallow some saliva, and eventually feel the burning sensation in my chest subside.

Footsteps.

A door creaks. My heart drops like it's fallen from a twelve-story building. I wait, expecting a strong shove. A heaviness falls over me as I dart my gaze around in several directions. Thunder rumbles outside as a storm lurks in closer, seemingly aware of the Boogeyman's impending arrival.

Maybe I can break one of the windows and scream for help? Maybe I—

A sudden movement off to the side sends chills lynching the flesh off my bones. I wheel around. A pale blue curtain billows in the wind a few feet away from me, dancing with the gust of the rain. I put the knife in my waistband and step closer to the window, feeling the cool breeze against my chest and face. A moment later, a door swings open, bumping against its jamb.

"You put on quite a show. I'm impressed."

A flash of lightning illuminates the room in front of me.

The white mask grins at me.

Silhouetted by the cold fluorescent porch light that penetrates the doorway is my hunter. He enters the kitchen, humming a tune under his breath.

I don't have time to move.

I don't have time to reach for the knife behind me, much less hold it up.

I don't have time to scream.

Before I can make any movement, he buries his fist into my gut, vacuuming the air from my lungs. He grabs me from behind and locks me in a chokehold. My pulse pounds in my temples as my breathing is cut short by the pressure applied to my throat. He grabs me by the hair and jerks my head back.

"Bet you thought you pulled a fast one on me now, did ya?"

Every muscle in my body throbs. Black dots form in my eyes. He grabs my arm and drives me gut-first into the kitchen island, knocking the wind out of me. He then flings me to the ground so hard my head bounces off the floor.

I curl up into a ball, hugging myself in a fetal position, begging for all this to end.

"The game may be over, but that doesn't mean we don't get to have fun anymore."

I don't respond.

At that moment, he raises his foot above me and rams it down onto my shoulder. Something snaps as I scream. He picks me up by the hair and flings me against the wall. I fall backward, crashing into the weak plaster. The impact jolts me, then the sickening pain comes all at once.

The man chuckles under the mask.

"I was looking to get rid of Sadie, actually. She's been making demands. Wanting me to live with her. I have a wife, you see, and it's my job to make that bitch think I care about her. Sadie, well, she was just fun to be around. I'd make her ask suckers for help on the street, get them to her car, where I'd be waiting in the back seat to chloroform them. Your friend was one of them, you know. He was such a kind man, so willing to help out even the most disgusting, worthless junkie bitch. What was his name again?"

"You keep his fucking name out of your mouth, motherfucker," I rasp.

I try to push myself up, but he clamps his hand around the back of my neck and holds me tight. When I try to fight him off, he hoists me up and throws me down to the floor.

He laughs and lights a cigarette, then kicks the air out of my gut.

"You watch your mouth, you little shit."

He takes a puff from his cigarette and blows out a couple of smoke rings. He stops to kill his cigarette on my neck. On my elbows and knees, I cry out.

"Motherf—"

"That's what I like, resilience. Show me what you got, you little shit."

He gets on the floor with me, digging his thumbnail into one of the open lacerations on my thigh. The burning sensation digs into my muscle, eliciting a helpless yelp from me. He grabs my ankle and pulls my thin legs apart.

I look down at his crotch; he's rock hard.

"Yes, maybe we can have a bit of fun while the camera is off. Think of all the things I can put in you. Ever been fucked in the ass with a glass bottle, faggot?"

"Go to hell."

"I used to play around with kids like you a lot a few years back, before Novak found out about me. He likes recruiting the sickest people, you know. What do you say I turn you over and show you what I did to her pink little ass with this broken bottle?"

"N-no ..."

I didn't look up, didn't move at all, I just lay there stretched out, arm hidden behind my back. Waiting for an opportune moment ...

"I used to kidnap kids that were younger than you. I'd take them to secluded houses, hold other kids at gunpoint, and make their parents torture my victim. You shoulda seen it. This bitch named Lauren was one of my favorites. She really fucked up this Cody kid I found from a shitty trailer park. I'm talking ass-raped him with a dildo and skinned his face off before biting off his cock."

He kisses my foot, then begins to lick a trail of blood up to my inner thigh. He works his way farther, darting his tongue out at my crotch. It's slimy, like a leech looking for a snack.

"And then I convinced her own kid to shoot her, then took her with me. Rinse, repeat. Man, that next family really fucked her up. The things they did to her ... Not a single patch of her skin wasn't covered in welts. They skinned off her pussy and pierced her nipples with dozens of safety pins and killed cigarettes in her eyes ... Fuck, I'm getting hard just thinking about it. I know kids are kinky—I bet her pretty little cunt got all nice and wet as the boy's daddy pissed on her face."

He then clutches my ankle and pulls, hoisting me off the floor. With one swift motion, he flings me at a kitchen cabinet. My back hits the hollow wood so hard the top door opens and all manner of cans and kitchen appliances spill to the floor. Strands of brown acidic globs fly out of my mouth. I cough all of it out, the bread from his fridge that I'd just been in the process of digesting. I buck and whimper, but it's all for naught. I slide down to my side, slipping on the warm goo below me.

And then I see it. Right next to the pile of vomit, piled next to a series of cans.

A can of antiseptic spray.

An aerosol bottle.

"Hey, wanna see the tape of that guy you were in the tub with? I know he was special to you. Would you care to see how I held him still as Sadie sucked his cock? Yeah. She chewed on his dick like a good little slut while I poured acid into his pretty blue eye. Say, have you ever thought about sucking his dick? It's not too late, you know. You would want that, wouldn't you? You could lick his cold, dead prick. Suck that baby right into your mouth. Fill your mouth with him. How about licking his ass? Wouldn't you just love to taste where he shits? Shit like that is what you faggots are into anyway, right?"

He sits up and takes out another cigarette.

He plants it between his lips.

Now is my chance.

He takes out his lighter and flicks the flame open to light the next cigarette.

Fucking idiot.

I thrust the aerosol can at his face and squeeze. The plume of fire bursts upward, enveloping his entire head.

Thank you, Joe.

"Fuck! What the fuck! I'll kill you, you little fucking shit!"

His mask falls as he bats at the flames. Standing over me is a figure so deformed, vile, and grotesque, not even my darkest, most terrifying nightmares could've ever conjured something like this up. Its face an impressionist pastiche of fleshy colors, its one eye white and milky from the flames; blood oozes out of the burns as flecks of skin peel off.

He doesn't *look* like a killer. He doesn't *look* like the kind of demon you'd imagine if you knew all the terrible things he'd done. Save for the burned half of his face, he looks like any other person you'd see on the street. And who knows, maybe I have. He could have walked past me in all his averageness and I wouldn't have had a second thought. How many other demons lurk amongst us and go undetected?

He steps forward and raises his boot to stomp on me. Rousing my newfound strength and determination, I catch the boot with my one hand. My strength, of course, is no match for his. The sole inches closer as my arm buckles under the pressure. The gritty boot grazes my cheek as he applies more pressure. I twist sideways, making him stumble back as I rush to my feet.

Leaping at him, my jaw clamps on his left ear. His knee slams into me, knocking me back. Before I know it, his bulk bears down on me. Pain radiates through my entire body. Fear courses through my veins. He slams me on the counter, forcing the air out of my lungs. I sweep my hand to my back, grasping for Sadie's knife. My determination returns as my fingers wrap around the handle. He seizes my wrist before I can bury the blade in him. He redirects the knife to me, pushing it toward my eye. He could make me impale myself in one swift motion, but he's deliberately playing with me.

"Don't worry, I'm going to make this nice and slow."

Hard as I try, I can't overpower him. His strength and endurance seem to have no end. I shudder in agony as the knife breaks into the flesh of my cheek. This is it for me. I'm dead, and there's nothing I can do about it. Joe would have died for no reason, but he will know that I didn't go down without a fight.

So, what happens when I have nothing left to lose?

I open my mouth and push forward, the blade tears into the flesh of my cheek and grits against my molars. His black eyes widen as I bite down on the knife with all my might and buck forward, slamming my head into his forehead. I kick his gut so hard he doubles over, spraying a stream of upchuck on me. Adrenaline tears through my system, to a new level beyond deep, red rage. I drive my elbow into the side of his exposed neck. I shoot my legs forward. My feet clap against his chest with a loud thud. With a yowl, he tumbles backward and falls to the floor with a grunt.

I then seem to hear Joe's voice. *It's now or never, Dane. Don't let him get away.*

I pick up one of the hardwood stools, raise it over my head, and swing it down at him with all my might. He dry-heaves into the floor, gripping the red velvet carpeting of blood with one hand, holding his throat with the other. As he struggles to suck in his breath, I stumble to my feet.

I twist around and see him crawling, inching closer to me on his arms and elbows.

I lean against the wooden cabinet and, with an explosive force, heave it forward. The heavy wood crashes down onto both his legs, pinning him in place.

"My legs! My fucking legs!"

He twists and turns, thrashing up and down, but is unable to move. Air hisses from his throat as he gasps for all the breath he's lost.

"Who are you?" I rasp.

Before he says anything else, I raise the knife over my head and bury it into the crook of his neck. Unlike in the movies where blood splatters, his blood simply pours out from the slit in a black stream. I twist the blade, tearing into his flesh. A string of thick crimson jets out at me as metal severs artery. I then raise the blade up and bury it into his chest below his sternum. Again and again, I plunge the knife into him in successive, meaty slaps. Blood runs from his mouth in a slow stream as his movement ceases.

The rattle from his chest echoes around the room.

I stumble backward, gasping for air.

"It's over ... it's over ..." I whisper.

Chapter 22: NOW

I've been walking for what feels like hours. The sky over the wheat fields is tinged in lavender with the first rays of dawn. Factory smokestacks loom ahead, flanked by dimly lit houses. The sun rises higher, and the ragged blue-grays offer a shroud of fog to the unsaturated landscapes. The warmth of the daylight feels like liquid satin on my forehead.

Despite this, I know that a world without Joe is a world I don't care to live in. I have lived many years thinking I'd never see him again, but there was always that hope that I would. It was that hope that kept me going. That hope that I'd one day be taken back to a time in my life when I was truly, undeniably happy.

And now he's gone. And he's never coming back. And I'll never see him again.

"I miss you, Joe ..." I whisper.

I make my way toward an overpass in the distance. The road is empty this early in the morning, and there's nothing but empty land as far as the eye can see. As I stand on the edge of the bridge, there's nothing in front of me but open air. A few days ago, I would've second-guessed what I am about to do, but life has a brutally honest way of clarifying things. And so I take a step forward, into thin air, with no one to hold me back.

EPILOGUE:

"Yup, that's him all right," Novak said as he leaned over Dane's body.

He gave his men the command. They peeled Dane's corpse off the road and loaded him into the truck bed. When they arrived at the snuff house, they laid his body on the floor of the basement. His left eyeball dangled on his cheekbone; it strained to stay attached to a stringy optic nerve. A dried clump of blood caked his nose, which was bent unnaturally to the left. The skin on his head was cracked open, exposing fragments of shattered bone. His limbs were contorted in a fashion more suitable to a toddler's manhandled doll.

"Such a shame about Bret. He was one of our most popular snuffers."

"Can't say I miss that Sadie bitch, though. I have no clue why he kept her around. Slut was nasty."

Novak looked down at the beautiful specimens as if he were laying his eyes on his own children. Fixing his gaze on the body next to him, he savored the sight of those two for a few beats longer.

"Hey, boss, I wish I could've shot my nut sauce into the kid while he was still alive," the man beside Novak said.

"Don't worry, there's a pretty huge market for necro snuff porn. You'll get your wish."

Novak nodded at the two men in the corner. They knew what his vision was; they'd been working together in the snuff film industry since back when you could only get the stuff on VHS. They propped Joe and Dane on their backs, tilting both their faces to look at one another. Even in death, the two were inseparable.

"Camera's all ready, boss. We're about to start the stream in three ... two ..."

Novak nodded at the leather-clad star of the film.

"Start with the kid."

THE END

Printed in Great Britain
by Amazon